Brighton Bargain

by

Cynthia Moore

Road to Romance, Book 1

Brighton Bargain

Cover Art by *Tina Lynn Stout*

The Wild Rose Press, Inc.
PO Box 708
Adams Basin, NY 14410-0708
Visit us at www.thewildrosepress.com

Publishing History
First Edition, 2022
Trade Paperback ISBN 978-1-5092-3927-6
Digital ISBN 978-1-5092-3928-3

Road to Romance, Book 1
Published in the United States of America

At this point, the owner of the authoritative voice twisted around in his saddle, looking directly at her as she stood with a hand over her racing heart at the side of the road. The man carefully released the children to the ground, gesturing for them to follow as he guided his horse away from the ruckus on the street. "Observe what other damage can come of your rash actions. Your mother just experienced the fright of her life."

Emma quickly studied both boys. Other than flushed faces, bits of dirt and leaves hanging on their clothes, they looked unharmed. "What were you doing running out in the middle of a busy street? You are both old enough to know better!"

Evan, always accurate even in harried moments such as this, answered the gentleman without addressing her. "She is not our mother. She is our Aunt Emma. She doesn't have any children of her own."

The man grinned in a bold manner, his cobalt blue eyes glimmering down at her. "Dare I ask you, *Aunt Emma*, if you happen to have a husband?"

Dedication

To my number one critique partner,
my daughter Emily.
I love you!

Prologue

Summer 1818, London

Lucas reached out to grip the envelope with shaking fingers. A servant delivered it several hours before. He tamped down a surge of annoyance as he glanced at the handwriting and had tossed the missive to the top of the dresser, not caring to be infuriated by the words inside before joining friends for a few drinks and dinner at White's.

He contemplated his name written in his father's cramped handwriting across the front—*Lucas Carter, Viscount Millington.*

Grimacing, he flipped the envelope over, breaking the seal and unfolding the piece of foolscap tucked inside, while at the same time experiencing a contrary temptation to toss it into the fire.

Lucas,

Your mother and I require your presence at Watford House immediately. Because there has been no word from you informing us of your success in finding a lady of proper breeding and status to marry, we took it upon ourselves to secure an introduction for you. The woman's name is Lady Sophia Hampton. She is residing here in Brighton for the summer with her parents Lord and Lady Breech.

1

You are expected within days of my execution of this.
W

Taking a deep breath, he let the air escape through his nose. No need to fret. Their concerns about his ongoing bachelor status were not unusual. Admittedly, the note contained a slight variation in this instance with the requirement to meet a prospective candidate.

He stifled a yawn and stretched his arms up over his head. Tonight, excessive drinking and a tumble with his current mistress, Venetia, held no appeal for him.

"Are you coming back to bed?" She nudged a strand of her long, blond hair over one smooth, bare shoulder.

Lucas didn't reply. He contemplated her voluptuous, naked silhouette as she lay draped across the mattress underneath the silk sheets. Notorious for her exceptional beauty as well as the most talented soprano currently featured at London's famed Royal Opera House, men lined up in droves for the chance to bow over her hand in the green room after a performance. It didn't take much persuading on his part to remove her from her previous protector when he divulged the outrageous sum of money he agreed to pay for her exclusive services. She cost him dearly, but he had an irrepressible need for her company and her luscious body during the first weeks of their liaison.

This night's experience proved different. After drinking two bottles of wine, they climbed onto his bed for what he likened to a half-hearted bout of indifferent sex. Afterward, she snored loudly from underneath the pillows, a fitting conclusion to their unenthusiastic coupling.

He studied her for a moment longer as she gazed at him, while clutching the sheets over her bare breasts.

"No. I won't join you. It is time."

Her thin, rounded brows lifted over her azure-blue eyes. "It's time for what?"

"I want to finish this. It is over," he replied.

"But why?" She frowned at him. "I don't please you anymore?"

"I received a summons from my father to return to the family estate in the country. I must point out…," he paused, scowling, "…surely you weren't too drunk to notice the lack of enthusiasm we both displayed during our interlude this evening?"

She flushed, turning away. "I believed we were both tired."

He reached down to pick up his shirt he had discarded on the floor in front of the fireplace. He worked his arms into each of the sleeves, buttoning the front together before tucking the bottom fabric into the waistband of his trousers. "It is obvious we both lost interest."

She twisted around to face him. "Perhaps I should sing less often?"

"Not on my account." He sat on a nearby chair, reaching for his boots. "Why put off the inevitable? I avoided my parents' requests to find a lady to marry. I'm going to Brighton. I need to put real effort into the search for a woman to be my wife."

She sat up against the pillows. The sheet slithered down across the front of her sensuous body to pool in a shimmering cluster at her tiny waist. "You are going to get married?"

"It is a requirement of the only son and heir." He reached for his cravat dangling from the edge of the dresser, carelessly tying it around his neck.

3

"What will I do while you are away?"

Lucas frowned at her as he shrugged into his coat. He wished he could meet a forthright woman comfortable with herself who could divert him with intelligent, meaningful conversation. "You need to ply your wares elsewhere, my dear. I'm not so rich I can afford to pay you for services I'm not receiving."

She shoved the sheet off her body, swinging shapely legs over the edge of the mattress. "I certainly can't make do without the extra funds. Throw me my chemise. It's hanging over the back of the chair."

He did as she asked and turned to stare out of the window onto the street below. The rising sun cast a rosy, early dawn glow across varied building facades. The normally crowded thoroughfare presently exhibited little activity. He spotted a lone hackney cab in search of a weary, drunken customer. Three tomcats screeched at each other from a nearby doorway. Two women walked briskly along the side of the road. One carried a sack and the other held a bouquet of flowers. He wondered where they were headed on foot at this time of morning. Moments later, someone advanced from the other side of the street into his line of vision. A tall, lanky boy wearing a torn coat, tattered pants and no shoes confronted the two women, knocking the flowers to the ground before clutching the sack, pulling it from the woman's gloved hand.

"Confound it!" He sprinted to the door, yanking it open and bounding down the stairs.

He ran out to the road, heading straight for the women and the chaotic scene unfolding before him. The lady regained her hold on the sack. She argued with the lad while he pulled and twisted the bag, unwilling to give up his prize. The other woman stood nearby crying and wailing, making no effort to lend her assistance.

Lucas strode up to the group gripping the youth's wrist tight in his hand. "What do you think you are doing, young man?"

The lad dropped the bag and attempted to squirm away. "Please, sir, I don't mean no harm."

"The boy is hungry," the woman spoke in a firm, unwavering tone as she untied the strings and reached inside the sack. "I attempted to explain he is welcome to the bread if he will allow me to retain the other items. Here, take this home to your family. Let him go, please."

He studied the lad's grimy face and tired, blood-shot eyes. His tattered clothing hung loose on a skeletal-like frame. "Very well, one moment." He put his hand in his waistcoat pocket and pulled out a schilling and a few pence, dropping them into the boy's hand. "See that you never, ever accost a lady again."

The youth's eyes widened as he stared at the coins. "I won't, sir. I promise. Thank you."

Lucas watched the miscreant run away down an alley clutching the loaf of bread before he turned to study the woman calmly checking the remaining contents in her satchel, apparently unperturbed by the recent pandemonium. She wore a walking gown of lavender muslin embellished with three rows of flounces at the bottom, topped by a dark purple spencer and a bonnet covered with lavender-hued satin, decorated with tiny white flower blossoms. She finished her investigation and looked up. Thick, silk braiding ornamented the front her spencer crossing directly over her bosom.

His gaze tarried there in silent admiration of her lush figure before moving on to her face. Deep brown eyes studied him unwaveringly from underneath the wide brim of her hat. A strand of her thick, wavy brown hair had escaped during the tussle. It rested tantalizingly close on one smooth, lightly tanned cheek.

"It is none of my business, but would you tell me why you are walking on the street without a groom or footman in attendance?"

She pursed her full, rosy, red lips before replying, "You are correct. It is none of your concern. However, I imagine you came to my assistance with good intentions, obligating me to provide you with a brief explanation. I reside a few blocks from here. I received word early this morning a dear friend who lives down this street is terribly ill with a high fever. I am bringing fresh basil from my garden and ginger to her in hopes of abating it. As you can see, I am accompanied by my maid."

"Of course, I noted the quality of her assistance to you earlier," he taunted. "Allow me to escort you to your destination."

"There is absolutely no need," she apprised him with exasperation, sighing with great feeling at his provocation, causing her voluptuous figure to undulate enticingly. "My friend resides but four doors down."

"Carry on." He pointedly ignored her dismissal, sweeping one arm outward, indicating they should walk before him.

"Very well," she assented, "if only to attain my destination as quickly as possible avoiding further delay by arguing with you in the middle of the road."

"Wise choice," he agreed, not holding back a grin.

"What of the flowers, my lady?" interjected her maid with a sniff, indicating the forlorn bouquet lying in the dirt at their feet.

"Bring them. Perhaps we can refresh them with some water," she told her before striding away.

Moments later, they stopped before a black iron fence surrounding a two-story dwelling.

She turned to him with her gloved hand on the gate latch. "This is the house. Thank you for your escort."

"My pleasure." He bowed. She walked away from him and marched up the front steps. The portal opened at her knock, and she entered the house, the door shutting tightly behind her.

Chapter One

"Celia! You are the boys' mother! There is nothing unusual about taking them on an outing," Lady Emma Brenham declared with exasperation, reaching for her cup. She quickly took a sip of tea as she heard her two nephews' shrill voices from the hallway on the other side of the closed door.

"I am sorry," her sister, Lady Celia Dentley sighed, even as she continued to enjoy a dish of strawberries accompanied by a liberally buttered scone without pause, as if nothing as trivial as the loud voices of her offspring could interrupt the breaking of her fast. "I confess I often find myself at a loss when required to attend to the boys' boisterous habits. I derive much comfort from Miss Mills' presence."

"You gave her the morning off so she could purchase some supplies for the schoolroom. We promised Evan and Nicholas we would take them to the beach if the weather proved fine."

Celia looked up from her meal, tears beginning to form at the outward edge of her eyes. "I...I am afraid I'm not strong like you are."

"Nonsense! You simply need to remind yourself you are in control." The boys' voices were getting louder. She wished to curtail the discussion before Evan and Nicholas entered the room.

A moment later the door crashed open. The two

boys entered simultaneously, each pushing the other aside in a futile attempt to be the first one to gain notice. They spoke out in unison. "We are ready for our outing!"

"Good morning, Evan and Nicholas. You both need to greet us properly before we begin a discussion about our plans for the day," Emma advised them in a no-nonsense tone.

"Good morning, Mother, and Aunt Emma!" the boys called out.

Footsteps sounded in the hallway, and a moment later the boys' father, Vernon Simon, Viscount Dentley stepped into the room. "Good morning! Celia, why are Evan and Nicholas not attending to their studies?"

"Well, my dear…," her sister paused, looking at Emma with her brows raised.

She answered for her. "Miss Mills is in town obtaining additional items for the schoolroom. We are taking the boys on an outing to the beach."

"Yes, Father!" four-year-old Nicholas spoke up excitedly. 'We are going to chase the seagulls."

"That is exactly what I am concerned about, Nicholas. You and Evan will stay close to your mother and your aunt. I don't want either of you running away from them in search of wayward seagulls or any other unfortunate animals you may wish to follow," he commanded.

"But Father, we must be near the birds in order to chase them," pointed out Evan, the eldest at six years old, always concise.

"I will repeat what I said, Evan. You will not leave your mother's side even if that means letting a seagull get away. Do you understand?"

Evan frowned at the floor, mumbling, "I understand,

Father."

Lord Dentley squatted down, putting his hand under his youngest son's chin, gently raising it until he looked at him. "Do you understand, Nicholas?"

"Yes, Father. We will only chase the birds that are close by Mother and Aunt Emma," Nicholas answered in a somber fashion.

Vernon let out a shout of laughter as he stood up. "Make sure you do that." He glanced at his wife. "I must be off, my dear. I'm meeting Mr. Bins in the garden today to go over future plantings on the grounds. I plan to be back in time for tea."

Celia tilted her head to receive a kiss from her husband on her cheek. "I'm certain we will tell you many stories of our adventures when we return, my love. And don't forget, you are escorting Emma and me to the Seating's ball this evening."

"I didn't forget the ball. Please be careful today. I want all of you to stay out of harm's way." Lord Dentley looked at Emma with a glum expression on his face. "I dare to hope you can contrive to keep the boys' mischievous spirits to a minimum?"

Emma chuckled at her brother-in-law's perfectly accurate description of his sons' dispositions. "I'll do my best. I am certain nothing too upsetting will occur during our outing."

He pondered her words for a moment before replying. "Yes, it is too much to hope everything will go smoothly."

"Your sons are restless and inquisitive. One must be prepared for any eventuality." Emma flushed as she recalled the occasion she neglected to consider possible consequences, on the day the handsome gentleman came to her aid in London. She hoped her commonsense attitude would give Vernon a measure of assurance today. She watched the boys arguing over a leftover piece of toast while Celia sat silent, looking on their antics with a frozen smile on her face.

He turned to study his family. "I suppose one must do so. However, I confess I would feel much easier if Miss Mills were also in attendance."

"Do not worry. I promise to keep a close watch on the boys. I won't let them get near the water," she remarked with conviction.

Vernon pursed his lips together, frowning as he looked at her. She could guess his thoughts. A year and a half younger than his wife at twenty-five years of age, Emma proved to be as different from Celia in every other regard as chalk from cheese. Celia's fine, light blond hair, soft blue eyes and creamy white skin, contrasted with Emma's thick, dark brown tresses, and deep brown eyes. Because of her refusal to wear hats when outside in her garden at home on the outskirts of London, her skin tone could be described as golden, lightly tanned by the sun. Emma stood tall and curvy with a singularly large bosom; her sister's shorter stance and a slender frame even after the birth of her two sons proved a great contrast. Their personalities were diverse as well. Celia could be uncertain and wavering on matters of contention. Emma prided herself on a thorough understanding of her own stance on many topics. She rarely admitted confusion on any issue.

"I would never consent to this outing taking place without your presence," Vernon muttered.

She smiled at him. "Celia can find herself quickly overwhelmed in certain situations."

"To put the matter lightly," he responded, with a grimace. "Well, I must be off."

He patted each of his sons' heads before bowing to Celia and Emma.

"May we go now?" Nicolas spoke out as soon as the door closed behind his father.

"Your mother and I will collect our pelisses and change our slippers," Emma apprised him. "Please go with your brother and wait for us in the entry."

"We'll do as you say. You needn't worry. Worth will keep an eye on us while you and Mother get ready," Evan assured her.

Emma sighed as she imagined the chagrin of the Dentley household's butler when he became aware the two boys were unsupervised and left occupying his domain. She trusted Worth would be able to handle their impetuousness for a short time while she and her sister were changing their clothes. As she trod up the stairs to her room, she hoped their actual outing would not be fraught with a myriad of worries and concerns like the ones her brother-in-law alluded to this morning.

****

He made good time. The coach rolled into the center of Brighton just before dusk. Lucas shouted instructions to pull up at The Bedford Tavern. As the vehicle came to a stop, he pushed the door open, leaping to the ground before turning to address his coachman.

"Go ahead and take the coach to Watford House, John. Thomas should arrive with my horse within the hour."

"Will do, my lord!"

He shook the stiffness out of his legs and smoothed the bunched sleeves of his coat with his hands. Six straight hours sitting inside a coach never proved beneficial to one's appearance. He needed a drink and something to eat before he faced his parents. He stepped around a stray dog loitering near the door and strolled inside the tavern. He settled himself at a table by the fireplace, ordered ale, some bread and cheese from a hovering serving girl, when a familiar voice hailed him.

"Lucas! It's good to see you. How long have you been in town?"

He looked up to behold a tall gentleman with tousled black curls and piercing green eyes smiling down at him, a good friend, Sir Edward Collins. "Edward! Well met! I just arrived. Sit down, order a drink, and keep me company."

Edward quickly moved to sit in a chair opposite him while the girl rushed to the bar to obtain another glass of ale. "You normally never leave London this time of year."

He took a sip of his drink, relishing the cool, hoppy taste of the beverage as it slid down his throat before explaining, "I'm here in answer to a summons from my father."

"Something urgent?" Edward tossed his gloves and hat onto the table.

He grunted. "It is the usual complaint. My parents want me married. They feel I'm ignoring my responsibility to present them with an heir. They believe I am spending my days and evenings occupied with nothing other than meaningless pursuits of pleasure."

Edward stretched his long legs out in front of him. "The Earl and Countess are on that topic again, huh?"

"The two of them rarely stray from the subject." He reached up and put a finger inside the folds of his cravat attempting to loosen the fabric's grip on his neck. "I am tired of hearing their supposed concerns about the future of the family name and the stabilizing influence a wife will bring to my life."

Edward frowned at him. "Do you disagree with their sentiments?"

"It's not that I hold dissimilar views. I simply do not wish to be forced into offering for a young lady I feel no affinity for. I will not be content with a vague figure gracing the foot of my dining table. It is imperative I avoid the kind of life my parents live. They married without affection with little prior knowledge of each other. I am aware my father took a succession of mistresses since my youth." He pursed his lips, contemplating a battered painting on the wall of a frigate sailing on choppy seas before continuing, "I remember a time many years ago. My mother went away to visit her sister. I couldn't sleep. I got up from my bed and wandered into my father's chamber. I called out to him. A woman with a mass of disordered red curls and plump pink lips rose from the pillows, asking what I wanted. I ran from the room."

Edward sat forward in his chair. "A great shock to you, no doubt."

"Of a certainty; I couldn't understand why a strange lady would be in my father's bed. Upset and embarrassed, I never dared to ask anyone for an explanation." He took a hasty sip of ale. The serving girl placed a plate of chunks of cheese and a loaf of bread in front of him. "Help yourself. Anyway, you can't blame me for growing up telling myself when I married, I wished for something more than the *wedded security* my mother is always extoling."

Edward reached for a piece of cheese and pulled a hunk of bread off the loaf. "Are you saying you want to fall in love with a woman before you become betrothed?"

He studied his friend for a moment before replying. "To be frank, because of my parents' example, I don't understand what love between a man and woman is. I can't imagine or comprehend the emotion. Brought up by two people who obviously had no real attraction to each other, I suppose I would expect to feel affection for the lady I choose. However, I believe I lost my chance to experience even that."

Edward choked on the bread and cleared his throat. "Never say your father has decided upon a woman for you to wed?"

"He hasn't ordered me to marry her." He took a deep breath before continuing. "He wrote, instructing me to travel here without delay. Apparently, he has a lady of good family for me to meet."

Edward signaled for another round of drinks. "What is her name? Does she live here in Brighton?"

"Her name is Lady Sophia Hampton. She is residing here for the summer with her family at their estate."

Edward furrowed his brows together. "I am not acquainted with Lady Sophia. There is a good chance you won't experience an attraction. Could you stand being tied to her in marriage for the rest of your life?"

"The women," he snickered before picking up a piece of cheese. "They were actually no more than girls, who were paraded in front of me at the London balls for the role of my future viscountess, offered me nothing, no stimulating conversation or fascinating discussions on unusual topics. I did manage to obtain some paltry observations on the state of the weather. I'm hopeful Lady Sophia will turn out to be a deliberative, intelligent woman. I feel little patience or interest for the kind of silly, oblivious ladies I have met so far."

His companion picked up his fresh glass of ale and drank deeply. "You are content with your parents making the choice for you?"

"No! I will make such an important, life-changing decision for myself." Lucas swallowed a chunk of bread, staring at the glowing coals in the fireplace before continuing, "I'm willing to be introduced to her."

Edward picked up a chunk of cheese and put it in his mouth. "It goes without saying any one you would consider marrying must be of similar standing in society."

"Of course; that is something I would never challenge." He scowled at his friend. "There is no problem finding women to take to my bed, but obviously none of them would ever be suitable as my wife."

"No...of course not. They are entirely inappropriate!" Edward sipped his ale. "Speaking of mistresses, is Venetia aware of your plans?"

Lucas grimaced. "I let her go. She didn't entice me any longer. In fact, the whole process of getting drunk combined with late night half-hearted rutting for money has definitely lost its attraction."

Edward leaned against the back of his chair. "You resigned yourself to this?"

He gripped the side of the tankard. "What is there to lose? As long as Lady Sophia has a pleasing appearance and can carry on an intelligent conversation, my marriage to her has a better chance at happiness than the tepid, hateful relationship my mother and father live with every day."

"When are you to meet her?"

Lucas frowned at the half-eaten loaf of bread before looking at his friend. "We are to be introduced at Lord and Lady Seating's ball tomorrow night. Do you attend?"

"Need you ask? I will certainly be there." Edward raised his glass. "Here is to the successful conclusion of your search for a wife."

He held up his own tankard. "And to a woman who can interest and entertain me with her mind as well as her body!"

Chapter Two

Emma rejoined her nephews at the front of the house. Worth had the foresight to keep a few loose coins on hand for tips for delivery boys. Evan and Nicholas were busy rolling two half-crowns across the floor; each cheering for their coin to reach the distant wall first.

She smiled encouragingly at the butler as she noted the children's distraction. At that moment, Celia's fretful voice sounded in her ear.

"My maid couldn't locate my violet scarf. I settled for the biscuit-colored one," her sister complained, clearly preoccupied with her wardrobe and not at all concerned with her sons' activities.

Emma took the situation in hand. "The color highlights the dark brown trim on your pelisse. That scarf is one of my favorites," she reassured her sister, taking her arm to steer her toward the entry door Worth had opened moments before in some haste. "Let's see if James is waiting out front. The boys are ready to leave."

Her statement became a justification when Evan and Nicholas suddenly tired of the coin toss game and stood up, moving to the open door. Nicholas bellowed across the room as he sprinted away, "Come on, Mother!"

Celia languidly raised her hand to her cheek as she observed her sons race across the tiled floor. "Perhaps we should postpone the outing and wait until Miss Mills can accompany us."

Emma sighed in frustration. "You mustn't give up so easily. Evan and Nicholas are no different than any other boys of their age. They simply contain an excessive amount of energy that can sometimes be overwhelming to those of us who are not around them constantly."

Worth stepped forward to speak to her sister as they reached the threshold. "James has the young masters well in hand, my lady."

"Well, I must say that is a great relief. Thank you," Celia sighed as she stepped outside. "I had an image of the boys running out into the street and coming to instant harm."

Emma chuckled as she guided her sister down the front stairway to the carriage. "Your sons would never do something so foolish and rash."

A groom waited by the door to assist them. A footman stood in front of the horses and James sat securely on the outer top seat with the reins in his gloved hands. The boys' high-pitched voices could be heard coming from inside the carriage.

"Mother, what took you and Aunt Emma so long?" Nicholas demanded, as the ladies accepted help from the groom to climb the steps and enter the vehicle. "Evan and I waited for an age!"

"Your mother and I move with considerably less haste than you and Evan do," replied Emma as she lowered herself to the seat opposite the boys and smoothed her pelisse down over her broad chest. Celia settled herself next to her.

The groom shut the door of the carriage, taking his post at the back. Moments later, the horses moved forward, pulling the vehicle down the sweeping drive.

As the boys continued to talk noisily between

themselves, she covertly studied her sister who sat agitatedly pulling the strings on her reticule where it rested upon her lap. *Poor Celia, she never has the fortitude to deal with the boys' high spirits for any extended length of time.*

On occasions like this, Emma wished for a household of her own. Her periodic visits to her sister and her family were a pastime she certainly enjoyed. But the knowledge of the great satisfaction and happiness it would bring her to have a loving husband as well as her own children to care for, often occupied her mind on her sojourns.

Sir Charles Walling had shown a marked interest in her. For a time, Emma considered him as a serious candidate for her hand. Attentive and gracious, he met her as if by chance at many balls and assemblies. He arranged to join her and her aunt on several occasions as they strolled through Hyde Park. Their conversations and discussions were forced; not at all enjoyable or diverting. She soon admitted to herself she never recalled being excited or breathless in his company, the kind of emotional responses she expected to experience at the beginning of true, lasting affection. Thankfully, his attentions suddenly shifted to a newcomer to the city. Emma heard whispers from the gossips describing a plain, demure young miss. The lady's father was said to be a wealthy merchant. She believed Sir Charles married the woman. At present, no one else featured prominently in her life with the special traits Emma considered important in the man meant for her.

She studied the passing landscape outside the coach window observing an open, grassy area flanked by wide walkways. Several groups of people strolled along the pathways enjoying the warm, sunny day. She quickly examined the horizon to judge how far they were from the ocean. No sign of blue water that could potentially be cause for worry.

Without further contemplation, Emma reached up to rap forcefully against the driver's box. The carriage slowed, coming to a halt at the side of the road. The boys' loud discussion abruptly ended.

"Why...Why are we stopping?" Nicholas asked with a frown.

At that moment, the wooden panel opened, and James' peered down at them. "Yes, my lady?"

"I knocked," she spoke up before her sister could question her actions. "It appears there is a nice park up ahead. I wish to get out and take the boys for a walk."

"Right, Lady Emma. I'll instruct Ben to hold the horses' heads and come down off the box to offer my assistance in a moment."

"Thank you, James."

"Whatever made you pick this spot?" Celia whispered as the wooden panel slid back into place above them.

Evan studied the area outside of the carriage window. "It's just a pokey old park. We will never discover anything of interest here."

"You mean we won't see any seagulls?" Nicholas moaned to his brother.

Evan turned to look at Nicholas with a frown upon his face. "I've yet to see any kind of creature other than a horse, nothing but old people simply walking or riding on the pathways."

"Must all the places you visit contain a wealth of various animals and amusements, boys? I wish to walk

21

for a while and enjoy the warm sun. I see no harm in stopping here for a short time." She moved to whisper in her sister's ear. "Lack of entertainment is exactly why I choose this place. I judge it wise to attempt to improve our odds against any surprise or complication on our outing by picking a somewhat humdrum place for a beginning excursion."

"I suppose you are right," Celia sighed as she patted the loose blond curls at the nape of her neck that had escaped their fastenings. "I hope the sun doesn't give me any spots. Vernon does compliment me on my creamy, unblemished cheeks."

Emma stood up from the seat, thinking of her own bronzed face and arms as she reached for James' gloved hand after he unfastened the carriage door and let down the steps. She carefully wedged herself through the opening. Before stepping out, she turned to reply to her sister, "I think he would also appreciate a little healthy color on your skin."

Emma stood outside, her nephews sat still and silent in their seats while James helped their mother down the steps. Apparently, the noticeable lack of amusement provided at this park severely affected their rambunctiousness.

Celia thanked James for his assistance, strolling a short distance away to contemplate the trunk of a nearby tree.

"Come down, Evan and Nicholas," Emma called to them as they made no move to exit the vehicle. "I'm certain even this *pokey old park* will provide you both with some sort of diversion."

Both boys made snorting sounds in unison. Then Nicholas stood and shuffled his feet across the carriage floor to stand at the open doorway. Evan lagged behind his brother.

"Help me! Something landed on my head! Get the thing out of my bonnet!" Celia yelped.

Emma spun around in time to see a small, furry creature poke its head over the brim of her sister's hat. The animal suddenly made a hasty leap from the edge of the bonnet to land with a thud upon the ground at Celia's feet.

"It's a squirrel! We must capture it!" called Evan as he reached out to thrust his younger brother forward. They both scrambled down the carriage steps.

Startled by the boys' unexpected movement, James stuck out his arms to grab Evan and Nicholas to stop them from lunging forward into the groups of people gathered close to the carriage. Unfortunately, James proved no match for two frantic youths. The boys vaulted away, wiggling past the coachman in the blink of an eye.

Busy with the unenviable task of calming her sister down, Emma had no inkling of her nephews' actions until she heard James' cry of distress.

"My lady, the lads got away!"

She quickly turned around, gasping at the nightmarish scene spread out before her. Only moments before, several groups of people had been walking peacefully around the park. Now Evan and Nicholas were careening around them in a frantic attempt to capture their prey.

One gentleman, with his voice raised in irritation, complained, "I say, you scamps. What is the meaning of this?" Another red-faced buck, thwarted in his efforts to impress a lady as Nicholas sped by, bumping his leg, causing him to trip on the dirt pathway. "Just let me get a hold of you! See what you've done to my new pair of Hessians!"

Various ladies bemoaned the boys' actions. A regal matron started in surprise when the squirrel darted underneath her skirt. She made no effort to conceal her anger when her feathered quizzing glass fell to the ground. "You troublemakers will be made to pay! I'll never find another such as this," she moaned, as her maid restored the glass to her. The decorative plumes were noticeably battered and torn. "My son purchased this for me in France several years ago."

Emma called James to her sister's side, directing him to do his best to calm his mistress. Before leaving, she assured Celia she would make certain the boys came to no harm. With that pronouncement, Emma rushed forward to the approximate spot she last glimpsed the tops of her nephews' heads.

Miraculously, the crowd of angry people, that only moments before surrounded her, dispersed, and she made quick, forward progress. However, the harried image she beheld as she reached the edge of the nearest walkway did nothing to reassure her.

Evan and Nicholas stood proudly over the trapped squirrel. The hapless animal made an unwise turn during the chase. He was now wedged under a small crop of loose rocks with no avenue of escape in sight.

Nicholas spotted Emma first as she strode toward the boys. "We've got him cornered. What do you think of that?" he boasted.

"Look out! He's bolted!" Evan yelled.

She watched with horror as both Evan and Nicholas raced after the animal, heading toward the busy roadway at the top of a rise nearby. The thoroughfare in front of her was crowded with horses and carriages. She recalled the comment she made to Celia a short time ago, reassuring her that her sons would never do anything as foolish and rash as to run out into the street. It had been very wrong to make such a declaration.

"Evan, Nicholas, stop now!" Emma called out before uttering, "Please, please don't let them be injured!"

****

The door opened wide as he strode up the front steps.

"Welcome home, Lord Millington." Baxter, the family's long-serving butler greeted him.

"Baxter! It is good to see you," he replied with a smile as he walked inside, handing his gloves and hat to him before turning toward the stairs.

"My lord," Baxter cleared his throat in a nervous manner before continuing, "I was to request you to join the Earl and Countess as soon as you arrived. They are in the study."

He raised his brows in surprise as he turned around. "I planned to…Never mind. No need to announce me."

He strode down the hall and opened the door to the study. His father sat stiffly in the high-backed leather chair behind his desk. His mother lounged regally on a sofa nearby. He walked over to her, placing a kiss on her proffered hand. "Hello, Mother."

She gave him a frosty smile. "Lucas. It is good to see you. We wished to speak with you."

"Sit down." The Earl ordered as he pointed to a chair.

Lucas perched himself on the edge of the seat. "I need to change out of my travel clothes. Will you please make this quick?"

His father bristled at his callous comment. His mother frowned at him. After sitting up straight in his chair and puffing out his chest, Watford spoke through gritted teeth. "We wish to discuss our plans to introduce you to your future wife."

"No, you don't!" Lucas stood up, hands clenched at his side. "I agreed to meet this lady, nothing more."

His father huffed and gasped, coughing as he struggled to rise from his chair. "You will not bring shame upon this earldom and past Earls of Watford by uniting our centuries old family with a trollop you acquired on the streets!"

Lucas' blue eyes, which were the exact shade of his father's, widened in disbelief. "Who said anything about me marrying a *trollop*?"

"You told us the current crop of ladies on the *marriage mart* were unsuitable. You wished for someone you could be more comfortable with. What else would she be?"

He raked shaking fingers through his hair. "I am running out of patience with your insensitive treatment. I fully understand the importance of my position in society and the duty I owe to my family name as the future Earl of Watford. I would never go out and ask a demi-rep off the street to be my wife."

His father pounded his fist on the desk. "You give me no reason to trust what you say. You continually ignore both my and your mother's requests to become engaged to a fitting, eligible lady. Instead, you spend your days drinking, frittering money away at gaming houses and purchasing expensive baubles for your latest mistress. I put up with your stalling tactics for long enough. It is time we make the choice of a wife for you."

"I don't understand your attitude, Lucas," his mother interjected, with a sigh, "Surely you can see we are making the situation easier for you by choosing the woman you should marry?"

He faced her. "That is exactly the problem. Tell me how happy your own marriage has been? How many months after my birth did my father conduct his first affair? How many other men do you sleep with? Clearly you both botched your choice of a partner in life, why would I agree for either of you to make the choice for me?"

The earl's face turned dark red. "You speak out of turn! Marriages in our class are rarely love matches. They are respectable unions between couples from equal, eligible families. Once an heir is successfully conceived and delivered, it is quite acceptable to carry on discreet liaisons with others."

Lucas turned away without making a reply. He strode to the door, yanking it open. "Because of both of your examples, I can claim no experience with love in a marriage. I intend to treat my future wife with the utmost respect throughout our married life together, something you both believe is unacceptable."

He left the room without looking back, calling for Baxter to get a horse saddled immediately. He intended to take a ride in the park.

Chapter Three

Emma's heart pounded loudly in her ears. She took a shaky breath, reaching down to clutch fragments of her pelisse and skirt in one hand, lifting the cumbersome material above the tops of her slippers before striding up the hill to the street.

She gasped in surprise. Evan and Nicholas were each held fast by their coat collars by a gentleman on horseback. The children dangled perilously close to the side of a bottle-green colored carriage. On the seat of the vehicle, a corpulent, mottled-faced man frantically pulled on the reins, attempting to calm the animals as his horses reared and snorted their displeasure.

The gentleman, who continued to maintain his grip upon the boys' collars, spoke out in a firm, composed tone. His words resonated over the rumble of the carriage wheels, the commands from the coachmen, and the clomping of the horses' hooves.

"There will be plenty of other creatures to chase after in the garden at home, my young lads. It certainly makes no sense to cause yourselves great bodily harm over such a tiny squirrel, does it?"

At this point, the owner of the authoritative voice twisted around in his saddle, looking directly at her as she stood with a hand over her racing heart at the side of the road. The man carefully released the children to the ground, gesturing for them to follow as he guided his horse away from the ruckus on the street. "Observe what other damage can come of your rash actions. Your mother just experienced the fright of her life."

Emma quickly studied both boys. Other than flushed faces, bits of dirt and leaves hanging on their clothes, they looked unharmed. "What were you doing running out in the middle of a busy street? You are both old enough to know better!"

Evan, always accurate even in harried moments such as this, answered the gentleman without addressing her. "She is not our mother. She is our Aunt Emma. She doesn't have any children of her own."

The man grinned in a bold manner, his cobalt blue eyes glimmering down at her. "Dare I ask you, *Aunt Emma*, if you happen to have a husband?"

"It is you!" she gasped, suddenly recognizing him, the gentleman who came to her rescue in London a week ago. Flustered, she turned away to gather each of the boy's hands in her own. Only then did she face him. "I believe my sister and her husband as well as myself are indebted to you, sir, for your quick thinking and timely assistance in this matter, ensuring my nephews escaped unharmed from their wild and careless exploits this morning. However, I must remind you, we are not formally introduced. You have no right to ask me such a question."

The man stared at her, murmuring, "Still beautiful, clever and forthright! I didn't imagine it!"

Evan twisted around from behind her skirt to speak loudly, "Aunt Emma is not married, sir."

"Are the boys safe?"

She closed her eyes, sighing with dismay when she heard Celia's strained voice coming from the grassy verge behind her. Of a certainty she would need to comprehend her sons were out of danger, but Emma wished she made her appearance after the rather unsettling, forward gentleman left the area. Determining not to make a mention of their previous encounter, she opened her eyes and turned to observe her sister, accompanied by harried-looking James, standing several yards away.

"Yes. The boys are well," Emma assured her. "They deserve a harsh scolding. They ran out into the busy roadway, chancing severe injury to themselves or worse, because they were intent on capturing the squirrel. They were stopped just in time."

Celia raised a shaking hand to her forehead. "Evan, Nicholas! Have you no thought for your own safety or for your mother's peace of mind?"

"We should continue our discussion about what occurred at a later time," Emma advised her sister. The stranger silently observed them, listening to their discussion while sitting on his horse a few feet away. "James, please take the boys back to the carriage. Lady Dentley and I will join you there in a few minutes."

"Yes, Lady Emma. Come now, lads."

Evan and Nicholas walked slowly, with bowed heads, to join their mother and James at the bottom of the hill. Celia took each of the boys into her arms and hugged them fiercely before releasing them to James' care. Then she turned and took a few steps up the slope toward Emma.

"Is this the gentleman responsible for my sons' well-being?" Celia asked in an uncharacteristically direct manner as she reached the top of the bluff.

"Yes…yes, he is," admitted Emma.

The man nudged his horse closer to the edge of the roadway. He swung one muscled leg over the saddle and dismounted. "This lady informed me we haven't been properly introduced. For that reason, she is hesitant to converse with me. Perhaps you, madam, as a married woman and mother of two children, can perform the honors for us?"

"How utterly silly you are, Emma! I believe we can disperse with proper etiquette in this instance. For goodness' sake, this gentleman almost certainly saved my sons' lives!" With that admonishment, Celia turned back to the man, "I am Viscountess Dentley, and this is my sister, Lady Emma Brenham."

The gentleman bowed low at the waist before rising, studying Celia intently. "I am Viscount Millington. Your husband, Lord Dentley is an acquaintance of mine. It is surprising there hasn't been an occasion to meet you or your sister previously."

Celia wrapped her gloved hands around Emma's forearm and considered Lord Millington in turn. "My sons and I recently arrived in Brighton, my lord. My husband came a fortnight ago. I choose to stay in our home in Grosvenor Square in the city until my sister accompanied me on the journey to our estate here for the summer. We probably crossed paths without meeting in London. You must allow me to express my deepest gratitude, Lord Millington, for your quick thinking and prompt actions that saved my boys from serious injury today."

"You are most welcome, Lady Dentley. I am happy I could be of assistance. Your sons are good lads. They could be overexcited about being away from the confines of London. But tell me," he paused and glanced at

Emma, "dare I hope you and your sister plan to attend some forthcoming social events in Brighton?"

"Oh, yes! We most assuredly are," Celia quickly replied with a chuckle. "My husband promised to escort us to Lord and Lady Seating's ball this evening."

"Wonderful! I look forward to seeing you both in attendance then." Lord Millington bowed to Celia. Then he turned to Emma. "I trust your friend recovered from her illness?"

"My friend?" His whispered query caught her by surprise. "Oh, yes, she is doing very well. Thank you for inquiring."

"I am very happy to hear that." He reached down to clasp her gloved hand in his own, turning it over to rub the fragment of exposed skin at her wrist with his thumb. As she gasped in shock at this sudden, mischievous gesture, the viscount winked, grinning roguishly at her before moving away to mount his horse. He pulled on the brim of his hat to acknowledge them once more, guided his horse onto the roadway, and cantered away.

Emma did her best to ignore the warm, fluttering sensation in her chest as she watched the viscount's progress down the road. When she could no longer see him, she turned to her sister, "Surely you don't plan to attend the Seating's ball after the boys' rash actions this morning?"

Celia looked at her with brows raised. "Vernon will speak to Evan and Nicholas. They will be justly punished for their wrongful acts today. Why should we be denied an evening of pleasure because the boys were naughty?"

"Why indeed?" Emma commented in a sarcastic tone of voice, no doubt lost on her sister as they made their way slowly back down the hillside.

"Viscount Millington displayed an eagerness to further your acquaintance." Her sister squeezed her arm as they reached the pathway at the bottom of the slope. "He is very handsome; thick black hair, quite tall, a fit, muscular body and beautiful blue eyes."

She turned to study Celia with surprise. "You observed many details about his appearance. Did you happen to notice the condition of his teeth?" she teased.

"As a matter of fact, I did." Celia answered her query promptly, in a serious tone of voice. "They are very white and even."

Emma couldn't hold back the laughter that burst from her mouth. "The viscount must carry some flaws." Her skin still tingled at the spot where he rubbed her wrist. The roguish smile he gave her before he rode away could be a promise of flirtatious moments to come. The concern gentlemen only noticed her because of her large breasts reared its ugly head. But even with this uncertainty in her mind, she admitted to herself she looked forward to seeing him again.

"I do believe you are blushing, Emma! Apparently, Lord Millington has sparked an interest. You must hope he requests a waltz with you tonight," her sister proclaimed with much satisfaction.

At that moment, they walked around a cluster of trees and Emma spied their carriage parked directly ahead with James standing at attention next to the open door.

"Pardon me, my lady, but two aggrieved persons complaining of a broken quizzing glass and damaged boots left their directions with me. They are requesting some sort of remuneration."

"Th…Thank you, James," Celia reacted in a dazed

manner as he handed her the slips of parchment. "I will speak to Lord Dentley about this."

"Before we discuss the upcoming evening's events we must attend to the matter of your sons' punishments," Emma advised her, with a sigh as she had an image of her brother-in-law's probable fury over the morning's incidents.

Chapter Four

When his valet announced satisfaction with his
appearance, Lucas turned to study himself in the nearby
pier glass. He examined the snowy white cravat tied
majestically in the famed Mathematical style at his neck;
it bordered a crisp, white linen shirt with unobtrusive
starched shirt points resting at a spot just under his
freshly shaved chin. A classic white waistcoat detailed
with silver threads, slightly obscured an elegant black
tailcoat snugly embracing his muscular shoulders and
firm chest. His long legs were encased in black trousers
that fell smoothly to a point just above his black leather
pumps.

"You excelled yourself once again, Jacobs." He
turned to smile at his valet as he handed him his gloves
and hat. "I shall return late this evening. Do not expect
me before two in the morning."

"Yes, my lord."

He strolled out of his dressing room, deliberating on
the night ahead. He was eager to further his acquaintance
with Lady Emma. Other than her obvious beauty, her
actions and demeanor during the anxious episode with
her nephews were a good indication to him she carried
herself with the sensibilities of a level-headed woman.
He could think of several other young ladies who would
handle the situation with a loud, hysterical scream, a
swoon, and other antics in similar circumstances.

He reached the entry to find Baxter handing his father his hat and cane. His mother stood to one side, fiddling with the strings on her reticule. She looked up and studied him as he approached.

"My goodness, I must say you clean up very nicely, Lucas," she observed in a grudging manner.

"I shocked you with my appearance, Mother?" he demanded, in a harsh tone. "Your dress is lovely."

"Thank you." She frowned at him. "I'm not surprised at all. I see you so rarely. I find I need to remind myself of your features."

He raised his brows. "You grossly exaggerate the situation, Mother."

Baxter opened the front door and bowed. "My lords and lady, the coach has arrived."

"Come along, Son, we must not be late." The Earl growled the words.

"Thank you, no. I am required to call on someone first." He gave his father a piercing stare, silently challenging him to question the statement. "I will join you at the ball soon."

"Don't you dare drink and carouse and fail to make an appearance." His father clenched his teeth together, glaring at him. "We informed Lord and Lady Breech of our intention to introduce you to their daughter this evening."

A muscle on the side of one cheek twitched as the blood rushed to his head. His father believed he would be so crass and impolite! He took a deep breath to suppress his fury before replying, "Do not be concerned. I am resolved to meet Lady Sophia this evening."

"If you think you can…"

His mother gripped his father's arm, stopping him

mid-sentence as she steered him toward the open entry door. "Come, Arthur, I do not doubt Lucas will do as he says. There is too much at stake to ignore our wishes in this matter."

Lucas scowled at their backs as they descended the stairs and entered the waiting carriage. A groom shut the door behind them. He thumped his hat on his head with a grimace before pulling on his gloves with shaking hands.

Baxter stood behind him, smoothing what he assumed were imaginary wrinkles on his coat. "I trust you will experience a pleasant evening, my lord."

"Thank you. I certainly second that wish. I hope it ends better than it has started," he uttered the curt reply as he crossed the threshold and strode down the front steps. The carriage rumbled on before him, disappearing as it turned around the bend in the driveway.

****

Emma knocked on the door leading to the library, after Worth informed her that her brother-in-law could be located inside the room. She had requested her lady's maid, Mary, to begin the process of dressing her for the ball earlier than usual. She wished to discuss the matter of her nephews' escapades with Vernon privately, before Celia joined them.

Vernon stood in front of the hearth, staring down at the glowing coals with a glass of brandy in his hand. He turned to face Emma as she closed the door behind her.

"Ah, it's you. I hoped we could talk of what took place this morning before Celia appears." Vernon stopped speaking, appearing to study her attire. "That blue evening dress compliments your brown hair and eyes quite well."

Emma dropped her wrap and gloves on the seat of a nearby chair. She glanced down at her gown of rich blue crepe over a white satin slip, decorated at the bottom edge with a border of net lace. Embroidered with darker blue silks and chenille, the same lace also decorated the edge of the short and full sleeves. The neckline was secured as modestly as possible for someone of her size. She turned to get a glimpse of her reflection in a nearby mirror. Mary had created an elaborate coiffure. Her hair was parted in the center of her forehead, the long strands swept up to the crown of her head, fastened back in the Grecian style, and adorned with tiny, white silk flowers. A pearl necklace and matching dainty earrings completed the ensemble. "Thank you. I fell in love with the color when I first noticed the material in the window of the dressmaker's shop," she admitted.

"You look lovely." Vernon motioned to an overstuffed settee nearby. "Please sit down. Would you like a glass of sherry?"

She accepted his offer of a drink before settling herself on the settee. "How are my nephews?"

Vernon poured the golden liquid into a small crystal glass and handed it to her. "The boys are decidedly unnerved. They promised never to behave with such rashness again. The realization of what almost happened provided a more profound, sobering lesson than any daunting lecture I could give them."

She released the breath she had been holding and sighed with great relief. "Obviously, the boys didn't mean to put themselves in harm's way. I must admit, when I saw them race away toward the road, I believed they would both be grievously injured."

"I can imagine the horror you experienced at that

moment. Celia informed me Viscount Millington is the individual responsible for averting the unthinkable disaster." Vernon took a sip of his brandy.

"Yes, that is correct. I didn't see what actually occurred. I frantically called for the boys to stop. When I reached the edge of the road, Lord Millington held both of them by their collars. I swear my heart stopped beating for a moment when I saw they were unharmed. I stood still, attempting to catch my breath. I vaguely remember observing a gentleman nearby with a flushed face, attempting to control his horses from atop a garishly ornamented carriage. Then Lord Millington spoke calmly and firmly to the boys, pointing out the absurdity of causing each other great bodily harm over a small squirrel."

"I owe Lord Millington my deepest and most sincere thanks for his quick thinking and reactions," acknowledged Vernon in a somber tone. "He most certainly prevented an unimaginable tragedy from occurring."

"I'm quite ready, my love." Celia entered the room, her spare frame covered in a gown of pink satin over a cream-colored slip. The dress featured a wide border of pink tulle, and the short sleeves were covered with frilled tulle to match the bottom of her dress. A cap of pink satin held her long blond hair in place at the top of her head; matching kid gloves graced her hands and were drawn up over her elbows. An elaborately decorated shawl was draped over her arm.

"You look quite beautiful, my dear. I am a lucky man to be able to escort two such exceedingly lovely ladies." Vernon smiled warmly at his wife. "Would you care for a glass of sherry before we depart, Celia?"

"Uh yes, that would be very nice," she murmured as she gazed at Emma. "Mary did wonders with your hair this evening. It's quite stunning. You must tell her to discuss her methods with my Alice."

"Thank you so much. I will convey your compliments to Mary and ask her to speak with your maid."

"I would appreciate that." Celia placed her shawl on top of Emma's and accepted the glass of sherry. She looked up at her husband with a perplexed expression on her face. "I visited the nursery to say goodnight to our sons. They are very subdued. Whatever did you say to them?"

Vernon glanced in Emma's direction first. She struggled to keep a somber expression on her face as he winked at her, before turning to speak to Celia. "I didn't need to tell them much. The boys learned the best lesson by the experience itself. The realization of what could have taken place is a very sobering image, even to our young sons."

"From Vernon's description of their attitudes at present, I dare say Miss Mills will find her job a little easier over the next few days," Emma commented with a smile, hoping to reassure her sister.

"I confess their demeanors concern me." Celia frowned down at her drink. "It is unlike the boys to show so little spirit. It is almost as if they were ill."

Vernon chuckled. "My dear, Evan and Nicholas will soon regain their former enthusiasm. It is natural they should be subdued after the disaster that very nearly took place. I trust when they recover their mettle once again, they will behave quite differently and with caution if they are ever confronted with a situation like the one today."

"Well, that is certainly good to hear. You relieve my mind." Celia sighed and sipped the last of her sherry before placing the empty glass on a nearby table. "Were you able to sort out the two silly complainers who believed their items were damaged in the uproar?"

"I penned short notes to each of the distressed parties, requesting them to provide me with a fair reckoning of the harm done to their personal property."

"Most proper and generous of you." Celia gave her husband a warm smile. "Should we inform Worth we are ready for the carriage?"

Emma stood up, placing her goblet next to her sister's. "I am quite prepared to leave."

Vernon polished off the last of the brandy in his glass and then strode across the room to yank on the bell pull. Moments later, the butler appeared at the door and bowed.

"Will you please request James bring the carriage 'round, Worth?"

"Yes, my lord; right away, my lord." The butler bowed once more before exiting the room.

Vernon offered an arm to Celia and then to Emma, after they retrieved their shawls and picked up their gloves. "Shall we see what excitement awaits us at the Seating's ball, my dears?"

Celia smiled up at her husband as they strolled into the entry. "I trust any drama that might occur will be considerably less distressing than the upsetting event we experienced today?"

"Well, I would think, since our sons are safely in the nursery with their governess, you'll not suffer from anything as disturbing." Vernon grinned. "But surely you would welcome an incident that is more than commonplace tonight?"

Celia turned to face Emma, with a smug expression as their shawls were placed across their shoulders by the butler. "Of course, I would love to enjoy a memorable evening. Perhaps Emma will provide us with something we can talk about for many days to come?"

Preoccupied in pulling on her gloves of white kid, she paused at her sister's last words. "Whatever do you mean, Celia? Why would I give cause for comment?"

"Pray enlighten us both, my dear. What could you possibly be referring to?" Vernon stepped forward as Worth finished smoothing out a few creases on the back of his black tailcoat.

Celia grinned at her before she turned to her husband. "Lord Millington displayed a decided preference to further his acquaintance with Emma today and exhibited great pleasure after he learned we would be attending the ball tonight."

Vernon raised his brows and gazed at Emma. "That is astonishing news. Lord Lucas Millington is reputed a confirmed rake. He frequently comments on his aversion to marriage."

"No one said anything about marri…" she stopped mid-sentence, flushing as she remembered the viscount's pointed questions earlier that morning.

Celia placed her hand on her husband's arm as they turned to walk toward the open door and the waiting carriage on the driveway below. "What were you about to say, Emma?"

She grasped Vernon's other sleeve, moving with the others to the front steps. "Nothing of importance, Celia," she murmured, as she pondered the possible significance of the morning's brief conversation with Lord Millington.

Chapter Five

Lucas took a stance near the entranceway hoping he would see Lady Emma as soon as she arrived at the ball. He exchanged greetings with several acquaintances, but there was still no sign of her or her party.

A sudden lull occurred in the rush of people who moments before thronged the doorway. The hostess, Lady Seating, broke away from her position of honor and bustled over to him.

"My lord, the dancing has begun. Don't you wish to join the others? Are you looking for someone?"

"Yes, as a matter of fact, I am." Lucas glanced at the small, rotund woman, too late remembering her reputation for being a notorious gossip.

"Who is it?" Lady Seating looked up at him with her eyebrows raised; he imagined she held her breath in anticipation of his reply.

"The Viscount and Viscountess Dentley, Lady Emma Brenham!" the butler announced.

"Capital!" Lucas didn't attempt to hide his satisfaction when he heard Lady Emma's name called. He made a hasty decision to attempt to dissuade Lady Seating from gleaning any further tidbits of information from him. "I'm sure you are needed elsewhere. They will arrive momentarily."

"The Earl and Countess of Watford, Lord and Lady Breech, Mrs. Grace Wilcox and Lady Sophia Hampton!"

Lucas almost groaned aloud when he heard the second set of names. Lady Seating remained by his side with a sly expression on her face. Perhaps he could put the lady's overabundant gregariousness to use. "Actually, I am waiting for Lady Emma Brenham. I see she just arrived."

"Wonderful! Let us go and confront her." Lady Seating beamed up at him before she turned away; rushing forward to clasp her guest's gloved hands in her own. "Lady Emma, we have been eagerly awaiting you!"

She took a step backward as the lady gripped her. "Lady Seating, what…?"

"My dear, you are alarming our guest. There is no rush." Lord Seating advanced toward them. "Please excuse my wife's exuberance."

"George, go back and greet the others." The busy little lady looked directly at Lucas standing to one side of the group. "Come and join us, my lord. She is here at last!"

"Lady Emma, good evening; may I say you look stunning tonight?" He came forward and bowed low over her gloved hand.

"Thank you, my lord. Thank you very much." She blushed, glancing down the front of her gown.

"I said *you* look stunning. I referred to *all* of you," he clarified, with a whisper in her ear.

"Oh!" Her brown eyes widened as she gazed at him for several seconds before she turned away to gesture to the others. "My lord, I believe you are acquainted with my brother-in-law, Viscount Dentley. You met my sister, Lady Dentley this morning."

"It is a pleasure to see you again, my lord," Lady Dentley graciously acknowledged him as he bowed before her.

Lord Dentley stepped forward, bowed, and then offered him his hand. "On behalf of my wife and myself, as well as my sister-in-law, I wish to express our very sincere thanks for your timely assistance in ensuring our children's safety this morning."

He smiled at Lord Dentley as he shook his hand. "I am happy to be of service. The lads are adventurous tykes!"

"You are exceedingly kind; you offer a polite turn of phrase, actually meaning my sons are wild, impetuous creatures. I agree with the characterization, although at present they are as meek as lambs after their scare. But seriously, the situation could have easily turned disastrous with the boys badly hurt or possibly killed, without your quick thinking and intervention," Lord Dentley replied with a grimace.

"What is this I hear? Your children possibly killed or hurt? Whatever happened?" exclaimed Lady Seating.

Lucas swore softly. Both he and Lord Dentley momentarily forgot the presence of the meddlesome hostess. In a quandary how to get out of the turmoil, he observed Lady Emma move forward to stand in front of Lady Seating.

"You must introduce me to the woman in…in the dark blue turban standing next to your husband. I believe she is a…an acquaintance of a dear friend of mine in London." She spoke with a quick surge of words, forcing their hostess to attend her.

"Why of course I will present her to you. I must admit I am surprised by your request. The lady has only recently arrived in Brighton. She traveled across the ocean from her home in the States," Lady Seating trilled importantly before glancing back at Lucas with a wink. "You must promise me to rejoin your party as quickly as you can. I'm certain Lord Millington wishes to request a waltz with you."

He frowned as his quarry moved away. She effectively distracted Lady Seating, but now she would be in close proximity to his father and mother and Lady Sophia Hampton, the woman they were intent on foisting upon him.

Just as he resigned himself to the inevitable, making the decision to join them and request an introduction, a young dandy rushed up to the woman he believed to be Lady Sophia. From this angle, he could see the back of her head. She stood tall, with a vast amount of black hair piled up high in a thick braid. The frivolous man who charged up to her side, bowed low over her hand, beginning a rambling one-sided conversation. The dashing fellow waved his arms in front of him, gesturing wildly as he spoke. Lucas abandoned his previous intention, deciding he would be better served taking this chance to further his acquaintance with Lady Emma.

He took a hasty leave of Lord and Lady Dentley, making his way across the room to stand partially concealed from view beside a couple of large, decorative vases. Lady Seating was performing the introductions.

"Mrs. Wilcox, so good of you to attend our ball; I would like to introduce someone who believes they share a mutual acquaintance. Mrs. Grace Wilcox, please meet Lady Emma Brenham. Enjoy yourselves. You must excuse me. I need to return to my hostess duties."

He studied the lady in the dark blue turban as she reached out and grasped Lady Emma's gloved hand. She was stooped over clutching a cane, her still-becoming face lined with age. The feathers that decorated the lady's turban quivered as she tilted her head and smiled.

"It is a pleasure to meet you, Lady Emma. Please excuse my lack of manners. I believe it's more acceptable for me to curtsey, but those of us from the States find the practice a little awkward, and I am afflicted with a bad knee that wouldn't last long with the additional pressure anyway. Tell me, who is our mutual acquaintance?"

He watched with interest as Lady Emma's cheeks turned rosy. "I must apologize, Mrs. Wilcox. I told a falsehood. The situation called for prompt action. I wished to swiftly redirect Lady Seating's attention. I noticed your turban as you stood in the receiving line. I suddenly experienced an urgent necessity to make your acquaintance."

Booming laughter escaped from Mrs. Wilcox's mouth. "Wonderful! I like a young lady with courage and spunk. I met too many silly misses during my visit, so intent on society's expectations they lose their own original personalities in the process. I sense you dare to be different. You are unique, my dear!"

Lady Emma smiled warmly at the lady before replying. "Thank you for your kind words and understanding. Your accent is lovely. Where is your home?"

"I hail from the town of Baltimore. It is in the state of Maryland. Contrary to most residents from my country, I wished to travel here, visit my British friends, and enjoy the sights. I am staying at present with Lord and Lady Breech," the older lady responded. "Do you and your family reside in London?"

"My father, John Brenham, the Earl of Courter,

passed away a little over six years ago. My mother died shortly after my birth," she explained. "The house I grew up in has been inherited by a distant cousin. I live in the city with my aunt, Mrs. Ruth Turner. My sister and her husband, Lord Dentley accompanied me here tonight."

Out of the corner of his eye, Lucas observed his father gesturing to him. He must not delay any longer. He stepped out from behind the plant. "I hate to interrupt. I hoped you would dance the first waltz with me?" He bowed with a flourish before Lady Emma.

Mrs. Wilcox chuckled. "Of course, you must dance with your young man."

"He is certainly not *my young man*," she informed her without hesitation. "As a matter of fact, although we had contact briefly in London, we were formally introduced just this morning. May I present Viscount Millington? This is Mrs. Wilcox. She is from the United States."

"So far away from your home? It's an honor to meet you." He bowed to her.

"You are exceedingly kind, my lord. Please don't let me keep you both from waltzing," she urged.

He turned toward Lady Emma with a smug expression on his face. "What do you say to my request?"

She pointedly ignored him as she held out her hand to the other lady. "Perhaps we may resume our conversation at a later time, Mrs. Wilcox?"

"It would be my pleasure," she answered with conviction, as she clasped her gloved fingers.

Lady Emma turned to face him. "I am ready, my lord."

"Your excess of enthusiasm threatens to overwhelm

me," he murmured to her, with his eyebrows raised.

"I do not doubt you will survive," she retaliated, with a smile.

"Ah, the lady humors me. I believed you vowed to be forever disgruntled in my presence." He placed her hand on his sleeve, whisking her away to the far edge of the dance floor.

"I am disappointed," she countered.

Her blunt comment caught him by surprise. He cleared his throat. "You do not wish to dance with me?"

"Of course, I would like to dance. Forgive me, I am a devotee of plain speaking," she replied, with a grimace. "I looked forward to hearing more from my new acquaintance."

He bowed and she curtsied, he placed his left hand in her right one. She lifted her free arm across his right shoulder. He gently lowered his right hand to a spot on her gown just above her waist.

"I prefer to think of you as refreshingly direct." They moved in time with the music. "Do you anticipate an interesting conversation with Mrs. Wilcox?"

"What?" she looked up at him in a confused, dazed manner. "I apologize. I am concentrating on the steps. It has been some time since I waltzed."

He grinned down at her, charmed by the forthright, honestly spoken answer. Most young women responded with nothing more than titters or giggles, never actually reciprocating a query from him. "I inquired if you look forward to talking with Mrs. Wilcox."

"Oh, yes. Of course, I do. It is not every day one encounters someone who lives in the United States," she answered him, with genuine zeal.

"Quite true. I imagine the lady can impart many

matters of consequence to you about her country," he replied with a grin, charmed by her natural impetuosity.

She chuckled. "I am certain not all of our discussion will be of formidable topics. I would be interested in hearing about the styles of the currently favored women's clothing or the types of food they enjoy eating."

"Don't forget to ask her to describe the weather," Lucas added, hoping to provoke her. Could she truly be so unaffected?

"I doubt I will need to resign myself to such a mundane topic." She frowned up at him with a puzzled expression. "When one is actually interested in someone else's life, there is so much to talk about and to learn."

He steered clear of a boisterous couple who nearly collided with them on a turn. "I cannot imagine why I never met you in London or saw you at a ball. You do reside there?"

She looked away for a moment, appearing to study the other dancers, before turning back to answer, "Yes, I live with my aunt, in a small house on the outskirts of London. My father left the property to me. I experienced a season at seventeen, then again at nineteen. I went to a few balls last year, but I admit the endless round of parties and crowded balls never appealed to me."

"You surprise me." He raised his brows, looking down on her lovely, upturned face with a smile. "No need to dress up in your finery every night, to present yourself for inspection to the titled gentlemen looking for a wife, as well as the grand dames who are the arbitrators of one's hopefully sterling reputation?"

She pursed her full lips together, frowning before she replied. "You will think I'm ridiculous, but I must admit I dream of falling in love with the man I marry. I am perfectly aware, in our world of arranged marriages, unions are often made simply to insure the succession of the family name. It is a foolish wish, but I haven't lost all hope. My sister is married to a devoted, loving husband."

"She has a couple of handsome young sons as well. Come with me. I wish to speak more on this subject." He spotted a secluded alcove screened off by two potted palm trees while they were dancing. He led his dance partner to it, indicating a cushioned bench for her to sit on.

"You wish to talk about my nephews?" She settled herself on the cushion. "I apprehend they can be rambunctious."

He lowered himself next to her. "I want to discuss your notions of love and marriage."

The leaves on one of the palms that obscured the alcove made a rustling noise. His mother stood at the entrance, glaring at him.

"Where have you been?" Her voice shook with anger.

Chapter Six

Lord Millington rose from his seat. "Lady Emma Brenham, meet my mother, the Countess of Watford."

She stood up, curtseying to the commanding, regal lady standing in front of her with an abundance of silver hair swept up into a large comb on the crown of her head. "I'm very happy to make your acquaintance."

"Hello." Lady Watford barely acknowledged her before turning back to her son. "We require your presence in the drawing room."

He reached for her hand, placing it on his sleeve. "I will escort Lady Emma back to her family first."

The plant moved to one side again. This time a tall, older gentleman with a disgruntled expression on his face strode in the alcove. "What is the meaning of this?"

Lord Millington sighed before replying. "Lady Emma Brenham, this is my father, the Earl of Watford."

She curtseyed to the earl, a mature version of his son. "I'm honored to meet you, Lord Watford."

He bowed to her. "Charmed, Lady Emma. I knew your father, Lord Courter."

She smiled at him. "I am incredibly pleased to hear that. How long were you acquainted?"

"We served in Parliament together. We both sat during the sessions in eighteen hundred three until eighteen ten when we gladly returned to the seashore or the countryside to spend time on our estates."

"Perhaps we could discuss this at another time?" the countess interposed in frigid tones.

"Ah, there you are!" A gentleman with black hair peppered with silver at his ears wedged into the spot next to Lord Watford. "My wife and daughter are just outside."

Lady Watford frowned and pursed her lips together in a firm, straight line before glaring at her son. "Let us remove ourselves from this awkward space and join them."

Emma followed the countess out into the main room. A handsome woman with black hair streaked with gray, tall and slender wearing a gown of black crepe shot with silver thread stood next to a beautiful, statuesque young lady, with a smooth, creamy-white complexion and full red lips. Her thick black hair was confined in a heavy braid, secured on her head by a comb decorated with tiny shells. The lovely evening gown she wore was made of white lace over a cream satin slip, the bottom of the skirt trimmed with a drapery of silver material entwined with pearls and ornamented with large, pale pink roses.

The earl stood next to his wife. "Lady Emma Brenham, allow me to introduce you to Lord and Lady Breech and their daughter, Lady Sophia Hampton."

She curtseyed once more. "I'm very happy to meet you."

"My son, Lord Millington," Lord Watford added, staring pointedly at the others in the circle.

Lady Sophia acknowledged the introductions without speaking. Her unique violet-hued eyes homed in on Emma for several moments. Then she unfurled a little fan dangling from one wrist and waved it slowly in front of her face. "Uncommonly warm weather we are experiencing."

"Indeed." Lord Millington gave a blunt response. "I will escort Lady Emma back to her party. Look for me to return shortly." He bowed and turned to her, offering his arm.

They walked a few steps before he came to a sudden halt. "I must apologize for my parents' manners toward you. I am not excusing their actions, but I hope you understand when I explain they are presently preoccupied with, in their consideration, a profoundly serious situation."

She frowned when she heard his grave tone of voice. "I'm deeply sorry to hear of this. I trust the matter will be resolved soon?"

He grimaced before replying, "It is for me to determine. They are insisting I no longer put off choosing a lady to marry."

"Lady Emma, your party is looking for you."

Mrs. Wilcox stood in front of them, leaning on her cane.

"I overheard a woman, who I believe is your sister, questioning others about your whereabouts. She headed toward the refreshment room."

"I must go." She released his arm. "Celia will be concerned about me."

He stared down at her, a glum expression on his face. "I trust we can find another time soon to continue our discussion? May I call on you at your sister's residence tomorrow?"

She smiled at him. "Yes, yes, of course. If you will excuse me…"

Mrs. Wilcox put a hand on her arm as she turned

away. "I'd like to meet your sister, perhaps later in the evening?"

"Would you care to accompany me now? I will gladly introduce you to her," she offered.

"Thank you, I would appreciate that."

Emma walked, with Mrs. Wilcox tottering alongside, toward the room set aside for guests to obtain a light meal as well as a cup of tea, a glass of brandy or raffia for refreshment. She spotted Celia and Vernon sitting at a table just inside the doorway. Her brother-in-law stood up as she entered.

"Emma! There you are! I am in such a state! I didn't see you on the dance floor." Celia stopped her agitated discourse to pop the remains of a stuffed lobster roll into her mouth. She chewed and swallowed the morsel before continuing. "Vernon brought me here so I could catch my breath while he attempted to look for you. Thankfully, he almost immediately observed you headed this way. I am now able to relax and take a few bites of food. I confess I am hungry. You must procure something to eat."

Emma's head spun as she attempted to follow her sister's rambling comments. She took a deep breath, clearing her throat before she spoke. "I want you both to meet Mrs. Wilcox. She resides in the town of Baltimore, Maryland in the United States. Mrs. Wilcox, this is my brother-in-law, Viscount Dentley."

Vernon bowed to her. "It's a pleasure to meet someone from a distant shore, especially the United States."

Mrs. Wilcox's hearty laughter boomed out across the room. "It is an honor to meet you, my lord. Excuse me if I don't curtsey. Bad knee, you understand. I have been pleasantly surprised by the genuine kindness of the British people. I must admit I experienced some skepticism over the type of welcome I would receive after our two countries were lately at war together."

"And this is my sister, Lady Dentley."

"Surely you don't believe we hold the fact you are from the United States against you?" Celia questioned as she wiped her mouth on a serviette before awkwardly reaching out to shake the lady's proffered hand.

Mrs. Wilcox smiled at her. "I am happy to make your acquaintance, my lady. And no, I didn't think there would be much of an issue with my presence here, but I believed some consider me unwelcome."

"We are generally a country of decent, forgiving people," Vernon reassured her. "My country experienced initial discomfort with the speed of the United States' growth. Once we became aware of the unfairness of our attitude, Great Britain ended the trade restrictions and halted the impressments of American soldiers."

"Certainly, my lord; the leaders acknowledged their errors and did much to set things straight. I believe our two countries will eventually become great allies," ended Mrs. Wilcox, with a flourish of obvious emotion, as she swept one arm toward the ceiling.

"Well, now we settled that thorny issue, I daresay you must both be hungry." Celia was eager to change the subject, obviously bored with the turn in the conversation.

Mrs. Wilcox glanced at Emma. "Would you join me at the food table and advise me what morsels are not to be missed? I am quite ignorant about British fare."

Emma took a deep breath to quell the jittery

sensation in the pit of her stomach after the cryptic conversation with Lord Millington and the subsequent ill-favored introduction to his family. She determined to swallow some food for the benefit of her new acquaintance as well as to assure her sister of her continued good health.

She forced a smile to her lips. "Of course, I will accompany you. But our hostess has a reputation for her unconventional taste. I cannot promise I will be able to identify every item."

"Yes, Emma, please join Mrs. Wilcox and eat. It will greatly relieve my mind." Celia smiled as she rose from the table, giving her husband her arm. "Vernon and I are going to dance the next set."

"We will see you later. It is a pleasure meeting you, Mrs. Wilcox." Vernon bowed before leading his wife toward the ballroom.

Mrs. Wilcox smiled as they strolled away. "Viscount Dentley appears quite devoted to your sister."

"Yes, it was a fortunate circumstance for Celia to meet my brother-in-law in her first season. He puts up with her tedious ways quite admirably." Emma sighed. "One could say theirs is definitely a love match."

"Such a thing between couples in the upper class in your country is quite rare, I understand." Mrs. Wilcox made the observation with her brows raised.

"Yes, it is. Peers of the realm usually marry because they are expected to, not because they are in love and greatly value a special person they want to share their lives with. For the ladies, it is required we marry well by catching a wealthy, titled lord. The gentlemen are supposed to secure their property and holdings by wedding a lady of their own class who ideally will provide them with *an heir and a spare* as we call it here in Great Britain. There are rarely any emotional ties in these unions," she replied in a bleak tone.

Mrs. Wilcox frowned at her. "I detect you are frustrated with this state of affairs?"

Her new friend had quickly come to the crux of the situation. She hadn't planned on airing her personal grievances to others. She fanned her flushed face with her hand as she deliberated how best to answer. "I suppose you could call me a hopeless romantic. I am sorry for being so disgruntled. Let us fill our plates with some of the delicious food Lady Seating's august cook prepared."

Mrs. Wilcox placed a hand on her arm. "Please forgive me. I am certain you are aware the people from the United States are reputed for speaking out. Although I am a widow now, I experienced a happy marriage. I wed a particularly good man. I want you to understand, I consider myself your friend even after our short acquaintance. I am here to listen if you ever need someone to talk to. I will be visiting Brighton for another ten days."

Emma pursed her lips together, frowning before she responded, "I appreciate your offer. But I must tell you, as the years pass by, I have come to acknowledge a wish to fall in love before marriage is very silly and childish. Because of my foolish, romantic notions, I am left firmly on the shelf with no prospect of obtaining a husband or having a family of my own."

****

He had watched Lady Emma walk away from him with real regret. He doubted if there would be another opportunity to talk to her this evening. In the brief time he spent with her, he had known a wonderful sense of ease and contentment, something he could never recall experiencing with any other woman. Her interest in learning more about another country charmed him as well. He looked forward, with great anticipation, to renewing her acquaintance tomorrow.

"In here, Lucas." His father hailed him from the doorway to the drawing room. "We are waiting for you."

He followed him inside. Several tables and chairs were set up near the fireplace. The seats were filled with ladies and gentlemen playing whist. Much laughter, as well as a few groans from the losers, resonated throughout the room.

"I understand you brought your stallion from town."

Lucas turned around to find Lord Breech standing close to him. "Yes, a groom rode him here for me. I came in my carriage."

Lord Breech raised his thick, gray brows before replying. "So trusting of your stable hands? Is the horse not your prized animal?"

A servant carrying a tray containing full glasses of wine paused next to him. He took one. "I hired one driver and two grooms to see to my horses and carriage. They have worked for me for many years. I never question their performance or their care of my animals."

"Admirable, I'm sure." Lord Breech took a sip from his glass. "You must come to our estate and look over our stable while you are here. We own several prime goers. My wife is a bruising rider, always has been. She carried quite a reputation in her day."

"Arthur, don't give Lord Millington the wrong impression." Lady Breech joined the discussion with her daughter looking on. "Always at home on the back of a horse, I spent more time there than in the ballroom when I was younger."

"I'd say that makes me the lucky one when I met you on the dance floor shortly after I arrived in London, don't you agree, my dear?" Lord Breech guffawed loudly.

"Perhaps Lady Sophia would show my son the watercolors she painted of the area?" His mother wedged herself into their circle, addressing the lady.

"If he has an interest in them, of course I will." Lady Sophia gave Lucas a smile that didn't quite reach her eyes.

"Have you been painting long?" He pretended curiosity.

She shrugged her shoulders. "For several years. It's a requirement in finishing school."

"Is it not something you enjoy doing?" He wondered if the lady contained a pulse. She lacked an overall liveliness; her eyes were devoid of sparkle.

She pondered his question. "I call it a task to be accomplished in a day, letter writing, book reading, painting, and so forth."

"Do you possess the exceptional talent for riding horses your mother is gifted with?" he asked before tossing off the last bit of wine in his glass. He looked around the room for a servant. He needed additional fortification if he were to continue with this vapid conversation.

"I do not. My delicate complexion, you understand." She lifted her chin and fluttered her long, dark eyelashes at him. "It is quite impossible to adequately shield one's face from harsh outdoor elements while riding a horse."

"Perhaps Lady Sophia would like to visit the

refreshment room?" His father unknowingly came to his rescue from a discourse going nowhere.

"I'm sorry. I am engaged to dance the next set." She nodded to the young dandy Lucas saw her speaking with previously. The man moved to place himself directly in front of their group, bowing low. "Sir Raeford Crumby, meet Lord Millington and his father Lord Watford. Perhaps later in the evening I could be persuaded to drink a cup of tea."

"Wonderful." Lucas sighed with relief as he saw an opportunity to escape. He sketched a bow to the others while advancing toward the doorway. "I believe I will visit the buffet table."

Chapter Seven

"Lady Emma! Lady Emma!"

Her name resounded loudly inside the refreshment room. She turned away from Mrs. Wilcox toward the grating sound.

"Lady Emma! So happy to hear you joined us in Brighton once again residing with your sister, Lady Dentley," gushed an overweight matron, standing nearby.

"Ah…" She attempted to recall the woman's name.

"And such a coincidence. Charles is in town as well. He just arrived from London yesterday evening," the lady added in a strident tone.

The identity of the woman suddenly came to her. "Thank you for your kind greeting, Lady Parker." Emma turned to introduce Mrs. Wilcox. "You said your brother Sir Charles is staying in town as well?"

Lady Parker acknowledged her companion before turning back. "Yes, isn't it glorious, my dear? You and Charles may renew your acquaintance while he is here."

She experienced a sickening jolt in the pit of her stomach when she heard the lady's insinuating words. "I understood your brother married recently."

Lady Parker's smiling face underwent a sudden transformation. She frowned fiercely, her eyebrows drawing together to form one thick line on her forehead. "That woman played a cruel game with him! Charles made her father an offer, only to learn his daughter had agreed to become betrothed to another. It took my dear brother several weeks to rally back after such a great disappointment!"

Emma forced herself to ignore subsequent stirrings of unease. She cleared her throat before replying, "I am sorry to hear of his misfortune."

"Do not concern yourself any further." Lady Parker gave a broad smile, wiping a soiled handkerchief across her brow. "Once Charles learns you are in Brighton, I'm sure your presence will go a long way to help him recover from his loss."

"I fear you are placing too much importance on my influence with your brother," Emma protested, in a severe tone.

"Nonsense! But it is of no consequence; there will be plenty of opportunity to discuss the matter with him later." She turned away to gesture to a young lady standing behind her. "I want you to meet my daughter. She made her come out this spring. Annabelle, meet Lady Emma Brenham. She and your Uncle Charles are good friends. And this lady is Mrs. Wilcox."

Not wishing to appear uncivil despite her continued sensations of apprehension, Emma acknowledged the short, timid young lady who peered out from behind her mother's shoulder. "I am glad to make your acquaintance."

Lady Parker continued her vigorous discourse. "Lord Millington, you are acquainted with him? He was so kind to offer to secure some of the tasty tidbits from the refreshment table. Ah, here he is now!"

Emma turned to see the viscount, with his hands full of plates of food, staring at her from across the room.

Taking several long strides, he swiftly reached her side. "You see what happens when I play the role of the perfect gentleman?" he muttered *sotto voce* to her before turning to the others.

"I obtained a sampling of everything." He placed the brimming plates on a nearby table. "Allow me to locate a servant to bring something to drink. Excuse me, ladies."

"So kind, my lord," simpered Lady Parker.

After he strode away, Emma informed the other two ladies she and Mrs. Wilcox were going to visit the food table. They left the woman and her daughter to sort out their large selection of delicacies.

"Lady Parker is an overbearing individual," commented Mrs. Wilcox as they walked away.

"Oh, she is so exasperating!" Emma grimaced. "I am sorry common decency forced me to acknowledge her. As you accurately observed, she is very puffed up with what she imagines is her own importance."

"She certainly requires absolute control of the conversation," agreed Mrs. Wilcox. "Lord Millington displayed discomfort with the situation as well."

"Most people find it hard to repose in her company."

They filled their plates with many assorted items. Emma couldn't identify everything, but both ladies agreed Lady Seating employed an excellent cook. After they ate their full, Mrs. Wilcox announced her intention to visit the ladies' retiring room. Emma accompanied her to the partially concealed door, telling her she would wait for her outside in the hallway.

A portrait of several cattle grazing in a field hung on the wall. She studied the picture thinking of the park she visited that morning. She shivered as the realization hit her once again of how close her nephews had come to being hurt.

"Lady Emma! At last!"

She turned around with a gasp, her arm clutched by clammy, groping hands. "What… Sir Charles? Whatever are you doing? Unhand me this moment!"

He tugged her down the narrow hallway. "I need to speak to you."

She attempted to pull her arm out of his tight grip, but the effort proved futile. His brute strength overpowered her. "Please stop. There is no need to act in this frantic manner."

He ignored her plea. "We are going to talk. What better place than the secluded balcony overlooking the garden?"

Light-headed and out of breath, she attempted to keep her balance while he continued to drag her forward. "Pl…please, this is n…not appropriate. A…anything you need to s…say to me can be done with o…others in the vicinity."

"I beg to differ." He turned to sneer at her. "You led me on a merry dance when I showed an interest in you in London. You secretly want me. I simply plan to give you what you wish for. A kiss or two and maybe a squeeze of those luscious breasts of yours through that thin gown you are wearing should tide us both over for now. We will be married within a few days by special license."

"W…what are you talking about?" She coughed. "I have absolutely no desire to marry you! I never encouraged you! A couple of ch…chance meetings, a walk in the park with m…my aunt accompanying us. We…we danced together at a few balls."

He did not reply. They reached an open door leading outside. Cool evening air rushed out into the hallway. She groaned as she suddenly realized she dared not scream or call for assistance. She ran the risk of being forced to marry Sir Charles if they were caught together in this very inappropriate situation. She glimpsed a wide balcony overlooking the darkened garden below and planted her feet firmly on the carpeted floor in a last-minute attempt to stay inside the house.

Her Herculean effort made no impression on Sir Charles. He pulled her onto the outdoor platform, his strength and determination too great for her to counter.

"Let us make up for lost time." He dropped her hands, reaching behind to pull her toward him while squeezing her bottom. Then he moved to the front of her gown, fumbling and grasping at her bodice before he tore the material, exposing the side of one breast. He made a grunting noise in his throat as he reached out, groping the torn satin with quivering fingers to pinch her nipple.

She struggled to breathe. The horrifying tableau encompassing her suddenly blackened as she lost her sight. Her knees buckled, causing her to stumble against him. He clutched the ragged edge of the gown, holding her in place while he continued to squeeze and fondle her breast. She choked, panting for air.

"What the devil?"

Emma heard the startled exclamation the same moment her captor released her. Staggering forward, she blindly reached out, locating the stone railing with trembling hands, greedily gulping the cool night air. She closed and opened her eyes several times before she could make out muted shapes of trees in front of her. She turned around to see Lord Millington standing directly behind Sir Charles, gripping his shoulders with his hands. Then he squeezed her assailant's arms until the viscount's knuckles bulged and whitened with the sheer power of his hold.

Sir Charles staggered backward to land against Lord Millington's chest. The viscount pivoted him around until he faced him. He slammed his fist into his nose. With a groan, Sir Charles fell to the ground, flat on his face. Then Lord Millington placed his heel on his back. She watched the unimaginable scene unfold before her in a daze, while leaning backward against the balustrade. She took deep breaths to calm her racing heart, as she grasped the frayed ends of her bodice together in an attempt to cover herself.

"When I release you, I want you to stand up and apologize to Lady Emma for your extremely callous treatment of her. Then you will get on your horse or climb in your carriage, whatever type of conveyance you used to arrive here, and leave Brighton immediately!" Lord Millington commanded.

Sir Charles sputtered and sneezed. Blood oozed from his nose and from his mouth pressed against the ground. "I…I won't leave. I…I need to finish my business here."

"Whatever task or enterprise you came here for no longer exists. Do you understand me?" Lord Millington glared down at him.

"Yes…yes, I comprehend you, man," sniffed Sir Charles. "But you are wrong. I have business with Lady Emma."

"Viscount Millington to you. I did not catch your title."

"I didn't offer you any," Sir Charles spat out in an

insolent manner. He coughed. "Let me up. I need my handkerchief."

The viscount ignored his captive's demand, turning to Emma while keeping his foot wedged on Sir Charles' back. "Who is this person? Did he hurt you?"

She clutched her gown. "He ripped open the front of my dress and touched me in a most inappropriate manner."

"You swine! You blackguard!" A forbidding vehemence contorted Lord Millington's face. He shrugged out of his coat, tossing it to her. "Such callous treatment is unforgivable!"

"Thank you." She clutched the garment with shaking hands, holding it up in front of her like a shield. "The culprit is Sir Charles Walling. His sister is Lady Parker."

His brows rose when she said the names. He paused to clear his throat. "Indeed. Are you aware of the nature of the matter he wishes to resolve?"

She took a deep, unsteady breath before answering. "He told me he means to marry me. I hold absolutely no desire to do so, nor did I ever give encouragement for him to believe otherwise. Sir Charles and I are mere acquaintances, nothing more."

The viscount frowned down upon his fidgeting captive. "Not only are your actions physically hurtful to Lady Emma, but they are also entirely uncalled for as well. The lady has no interest in your offer of marriage."

Sir Charles snorted. "She is teasing me. She wanted, even craved my attentions when we were together in London. I intend to marry her. I will not be thwarted!"

Emma clutched at the coat and cried out, "Please, what you say is untrue. I never, ever expressed any intention to become betrothed to you!"

"You were not required to say anything. All the evidence I needed I observed in your actions, coy miss as you are." He rose on his elbows, spitting some blood on the ground before wiping his mouth with the back of his hand.

"My patience is wearing extremely thin." Lord Millington pressed his heel even further into the center of his victim's shoulder blades, causing his quarry to fall back down and his head to smack on the hard ground. "This lady *doth protest too much* as the Bard would say. I believe you are either lying or imagining her interest. Once again, I command you to leave Brighton straight away!"

Sir Charles snickered from the side of his bloodied mouth. "Pray, what is your interest in her, my lord? Of course, her breasts are large and enticing, but surely the more sophisticated widows or beautiful opera singers are more your style?"

The viscount didn't favor him with a reply. He reached down, grabbing the belligerent man by his coat collar before standing him up, pulling him inside the doorway. He called out to her before disappearing from view, "Wait here for me. I promise to return momentarily."

****

Lucas experienced a surge of anger greater than he had ever known. He forced himself to take a deep breath as he dragged protesting and bloodied Sir Charles down the hallway. His stomach clenched and he swallowed bile as he thought about the outrageous, abominable spectacle he observed when he stepped out on the balcony minutes earlier. He couldn't imagine the appalling, frightening images going through Lady Emma's mind. He must return to her as quickly as possible.

They reached the end of the hallway. A staircase appeared ahead with a door at the bottom. He fervently hoped it led outside to the back of the house. He yanked on the man's arm as he jerked and pulled, attempting to break his hold. The ends of Sir Charles' soiled cravat hung loose and dangling in two uneven, floppy strands from his neck. Lucas grabbed the pieces with his free hand and twisted the material until he formed a secure wad wrapped tightly around the miscreant's neck. "Don't you dare endeavor to escape! I will not be opposed. You leave the city tonight!"

Sir Charles snorted and gasped, obviously struggling for air. "I...I did nothing wrong. I understand her. She is shy. She needs some...some coaxing. I could have brought her around in a few moments without your...your appearance on the scene to interrupt my efforts."

The blood rushed to his head when he heard those pompous words. The pressure at the back of his eyes was so intense, he shook his head back and forth and blinked several times to relieve the pain. He didn't trust himself to remain outwardly calm for much longer; the need to commit murder was certainly not far from his consciousness. Without speaking, he charged down the remaining steps, pulling Sir Charles alongside. He thrust the door open, gratified to see it led directly out to the street.

A man dressed in some sort of official uniform stood a short distance away, arguing with a couple of youths who were brandishing large sticks. Lucas shut the door with a bang, dragging Sir Charles forward.

The man turned toward them when he heard the commotion and the two youths bolted away into the nearby woods.

"Come back here, you scamps!" the man swore under his breath, turning back to them with a scowl on his face. "See what you've done? Bother! I'm Mr. White, the local magistrate. Is there a problem?"

"You are just the person I wanted to see," Lucas remarked, with relief. "This scoundrel has accosted a lady, who shall remain nameless, at the ball taking place in this house. I want him escorted from Brighton at once."

The heavy-set magistrate shuffled forward peering at Sir Charles. "It looks as if he's met with an accident, man. What's to make me believe you?"

Lucas drew himself up to his full height tightening his grip on his captive's arm. "I am Viscount Millington. I punched this person in the nose for an extremely good reason. He is getting off lightly by being banished from the city, I assure you."

The surly man's attitude changed noticeably when he heard his title. "Yes, my lord, I'll see to it right away, my lord. My carriage is parked just up the road here. Come with me, you bugger!"

"You haven't heard the last of this. I garner influence in high places," Sir Charles threatened, spewing the words as the magistrate led him away.

Lucas ignored him and quickly made his way back to the house. Once inside, he sprinted up the stairs to the balcony. He needed to ascertain Lady Emma would recover from the night's unfortunate events.

She stood where he left her, leaning against the

balustrade with his coat draped over her shoulders, staring out into the darkened garden below. His footsteps resonated on the balcony's hard surface, and she turned to face him.

"I have sent Sir Charles on his way. He'll not bother you again." He reached out to gently cup her face. "I am deeply sorry he hurt you. I should have been here earlier to protect you."

She made a whimpering noise in her throat, twisting toward him so he cradled her cheek in his hand. "How could you comprehend he would do such a cruel thing? I am acquainted with him. I cannot explain the reason he acted so rashly. Thank you so much for saving me. For the second time today, I am extremely grateful for your presence."

Lucas took his hand away from her face, wrapping both of his arms across her back, pulling her toward him. Even through the thick fabric on his coat, he became conscious of the warmth of her body and the sensual weight of her breasts as they made contact with his chest. He caught a whiff of a light, lemony scent as he hugged her.

She took a ragged breath and sniffed. "Oh, I am sorry."

He reached into his waistcoat pocket, but it was empty. "Drat! I apologize. I am unable to offer you my handkerchief. I dropped it somewhere during the scuffle."

She slowly shifted in his arms to gaze up at him. "No. You...You misunderstand. Your cologne-I was relishing the aroma...it has a spicy, musky fragrance. What is it?"

He paused, momentarily taken aback by her erotic

words before he remembered hearing of intense emotional needs in some people immediately after suffering abuse. He bent over to murmur his reply, her full lips just inches away from his own. "It's sandalwood, no doubt also combined with the earthy odor of my sweat, considering the recent brawl I was involved in."

She sighed and snuggled against his neck. The silken strands of her hair brushed the sensitive skin there. "I feel wonderfully protected, at peace in your arms."

"Well! I believed I scented romance in the air!"

He quickly lowered his arms from her shoulders as he heard the high-pitched voice of their hostess. Emma stepped away from him. He turned to face Lady Seating's triumphant smile.

"You misunderstand the situation," he informed her in a grave, serious tone. "I am comforting Lady Emma, a victim of a grievously insensitive attack by one of your guests."

Lady Seating's smile froze on her face. "By one of *my* guests? Tell me who has done such a thing?"

"Did you and Charles speak together?" Lady Parker bustled out onto the balcony with her daughter striding behind her.

Lucas walked forward. "Your brother has left the ball. In fact, he is on his way out of the city."

"I did not invite Sir Charles!" Lady Seating exclaimed.

Lady Parker gasped. "Charles has left? Why would he do such a thing so abruptly, without taking leave of me first?"

"He has gone because I ordered him to go," he replied, his voice gruff with barely concealed rage.

"Your brother callously forced himself upon Lady Emma. It is extremely fortunate I arrived when I did to put an immediate stop to his offensive actions."

Lady Parker's mouth dropped open in surprise. She turned to look fixedly at Lady Emma. "Charles told me he meant to ask you to marry him. Are you certain you did not misinterpret his intentions?"

Lady Emma stared directly at the revolting woman, gripping Lucas' coat. "Sir Charles didn't ask me to marry him. He commanded me to do so before he brutally forced himself upon me."

Lady Parker put a hand to her forehead while her face turned a beet-red color. "I...I don't understand. I must apologize for him. I will return home and discuss this matter with my husband. Come with me, Annabelle." She clutched her daughter's arm and they both rushed inside.

Lady Seating moved forward, side-stepping the puddle of blood on the ground, intently studying Lady Emma. "This is beyond anything! The idea such a thing would take place in my home to one of my guests! Whatever came over Sir Charles?"

"Emma, Emma, what has happened?" Lady Dentley hastened outside with her husband following closely behind her.

Lord Dentley walked around his wife confronting his sister-in-law, his expression grave. "What can we do for you, Emma?"

Lucas noticed her shivering in the chilly night air and spoke out, "Please escort her to your home immediately. She needs to rest. The entire story can be related to you both in the morning."

Chapter Eight

After the short ride to the Dentley estate, Emma exited the vehicle, solicitously helped from the carriage by her brother-in-law as well as a groom and a footman. Her shawl was draped securely across her chest, her torn gown haphazardly pinned in place, Lord Millington's coat returned to him. She ascended the front steps with Vernon at her side and Celia leading the way; her sister continually turning around to check on their progress. They entered the front door held open by Worth to be greeted by Emma's maid, standing off to one side with a concerned expression on her face.

"We sent a note ahead letting Worth understand you were taken ill," Vernon spoke softly in Emma's ear as he handed her over to Mary, who took her arm and helped her up the stairs to her room. Once safely inside the chamber, her jewelry, ruined gown, and undergarments were taken off with her maid's careful assistance.

"My lady! Whatever happened?" Mary gasped as she gently removed Emma's chemise.

"What is wrong?" Emma exclaimed, turning to study her naked torso in the mirror. A dark purple bruise formed in the shape of a finger across the side of her right breast. She tiredly gave Mary a condensed account of what happened at the ball.

Her maid grimaced when she finished the story. "The man is a monster, my lady."

Emma's hair was brushed; a cloth dipped in warm water soothed her tender breast. Finally, Mary lowered a soft cotton night rail over her head and handed her a clean shawl.

A knock sounded upon the door.

"Yes?" Emma called out, as she wrapped the warm garment across her shoulders.

"It is Celia, my dear." The door opened a crack. "I am worried about you. May I come in?"

She sighed with fatigue. She had told Celia and Vernon an abbreviated version of what occurred with Sir Charles as they were returning home in the carriage. All she wished to do at this moment was to make an attempt to get her mind off the horrifying incident. No doubt her sister wanted to hear additional details. "Yes, you may. I planned to read for a short while before I went to bed. Mary, will you bring me a cup of tea? Would you like a cup as well, Celia?"

"No, thank you."

"I'll get the tea for you right away, my lady." Her maid curtseyed and left the room.

Celia frowned at her as the chamber door closed. "Any ideas why Sir Charles acted the way he did tonight?"

Emma pulled her shawl across her chest and sat down on the overstuffed settee in the corner of the room. She gave her sister a weary smile and patted the spot next to her. "I am shocked by what happened, but I have come up with a possibility. While it is certainly no excuse for his hurtful actions, I believe he is frustrated by his recent failure to secure a wealthy bride."

Celia sat down, appearing to ponder her words. "What makes you think such a thing? Why would he treat you in such a brutish manner?"

She turned to stare at the glowing coals in the fireplace for a moment before answering. "Are you aware of the cruel remarks men have made about my br…breasts?"

Her sister gasped. "No!"

She took a deep breath. "I have been called 'Busty Brenham' and 'Brenham the Barge,' to give you a sampling. The distressing comments have been a detriment as well as a source of embarrassment to me. I find it impossible to believe a gentleman genuinely enjoys my company. I assume they have a fascination for my br…breasts. I suppose the fact that I possess an ample fortune is an additional incentive."

Celia reached for her hand, gently squeezing it. "Is this the reason you have never married? I am exceedingly sorry to hear of the distressing things that have been said to you, Emma. You are a lovely, smart, caring woman. Any honorable gentleman would be gratified to have you for a wife and lifelong companion."

"Thank you, Celia. I wonder now if those coarse, insensitive comments from others have caused Sir Charles to decide he could treat me without respect. I also remember the time period when he suddenly shifted his notice away from me last year. He became preoccupied by a wealthy merchant's daughter who just arrived in town. I saw no more of him. I believed he'd married the woman. However, Lady Parker informed me this evening he offered for the lady but learned from her father his daughter agreed to be betrothed to another. It is not far-fetched, after what transpired this evening, to say Sir Charles would become enraged if he were to be cuckolded in such a manner."

"Your explanation sounds plausible, but why should he now take his frustrations out on you?" Celia remarked, with a puzzled expression on her face.

She sighed before replying. "I imagine he has run aground; he has no money. The animosity displayed toward me tonight contained no justification. But it could be caused by panic. Possibly he believed marrying me would be a quick method to obtain funds. He harbors enough conceit to believe I would never turn down an offer of marriage from him. He is also aware I visit you and your family every summer. He learned of the Seating's ball tonight and assumed I would be attending with you and Vernon."

"Lady Parker no doubt informed him of the event even though he never received an invitation," Celia added, in a cynical manner.

"Of course, she did," Emma agreed. "If he is indeed suffering from money problems, he probably counted on my agreement to marry him by special license. He has the arrogance to think I am a lonely old maid who would jump at the opportunity. After we were married, he planned to take immediate control of my inheritance from Father, something he could easily do as my husband. To force himself upon me in such a brutal manner is certainly an appalling way to go about convincing me to become his wife. However, the desperation Sir Charles exhibited when he accosted me, tells me there is a good possibility he has visited the notorious moneylenders in London. They could be demanding immediate payment."

"Whatever his trouble, there is absolutely no excuse for what Sir Charles did or tried to do to you!" Celia reached over to gently rub her hand. "You need to tell

Vernon your suspicions as soon as possible."

A knock sounded upon the door once again. Mary entered the room bearing a tea tray. Vernon followed immediately behind her. "Emma is weary after her ordeal, my dear. We should wait and discuss what took place this evening in detail in the morning."

Emma cleared her throat before speaking. "I want to tell you both, there…there is a nasty bruise in ah…ah my chest area."

"What? No! Emma!" Celia exclaimed.

"I'm not surprised Sir Charles left a mark. I blacked out for a moment when he attacked me. I came to my senses shortly afterward to find his hand poking and prodding me inside my torn bodice." Her face flushed after speaking of something so personal in front of her brother-in-law.

"I will ask Mrs. Moss to prepare a cold compress," her sister told her, in a bracing manner. "You are aware our housekeeper is famous for her remedies; she has much practice with the boys' bumps and bruises. I am certain it would bring you great relief from the pain."

"I will request the compress be sent to you immediately," Vernon assured her before helping Celia to stand, guiding her toward the open door. He suddenly dropped her arm and reached inside his waistcoat pocket, turning back to Emma with a piece of paper in his hand. "I almost forgot. Lord Millington met with me a few minutes ago. He asked me to give you this." With that, he rejoined her sister, steering her out of the room and down the hall.

Mary shut the door behind them. Emma unfolded the piece of paper. Large, scrawled words jumped out at her from the page. Obviously, the viscount wrote with haste.

Lady Emma,

I requested an audience with your brother-in-law shortly after you and your party returned. I told him my version of what occurred tonight with Sir Charles. Although I assured you he had left the city and wouldn't bother you again, I cannot be easy until I am certain he has actually left Brighton. Lord Dentley informed me he plans to learn his exact location tomorrow. I offered my assistance and he accepted. Unfortunately, I won't be able to wait upon you tomorrow as I planned. Please accept my apologies.

Lucas Carter, Viscount Millington

****

Lucas sipped on a glass of brandy in his father's library, contemplating the glowing embers in the fireplace. Presently, after two o'clock in the morning, his parents had long ago retired for the night. Thankfully, because of his late return, there had been no opportunity to face their queries about his first impressions of Lady Sophia.

His pulse throbbed and pounded inside his head. A great many things had happened tonight. He needed some time to deliberate over the events before going to bed.

A knock sounded upon the door. He turned around. "Yes?"

Baxter entered the room. "Sir Edward is asking if he may speak with you, my lord."

Edward! He suddenly realized his friend never made an appearance at the ball. "Yes, of course, let him in. And take yourself off to bed, Baxter. I can see him out and lock up."

"Yes, my lord. Thank you, my lord."

Edward strolled in moments later, shutting the door behind him. "I'm glad to find you still awake. I am sorry I didn't make it this evening."

"Pour yourself some brandy. I confess I forgot you intended to make an appearance at the ball until Baxter informed me you were here."

A noise sounded on the door once again.

"Yes?"

Baxter entered the room and bowed. He carried a folded piece of paper on a tray. "This just arrived, my lord. I believed it might be of importance."

He took hold of the missive. "Thank you. Wait a moment, please. I will see if this requires an answer."

Lord Millington,

Your note tonight brought me much comfort. I too would feel very relieved to understand Sir Charles left the city. There is something important I want to tell you about my assailant. I have a theory, based on his brutal, irrational actions at the ball as well as information I learned that he recently failed in an attempt to become betrothed to a wealthy merchant's daughter. It makes sense he is in dire need of funds, possibly has visited one of the notorious money lenders in London. I trust this intelligence is of value to you. I will also inform my brother-in-law of my thoughts on the matter in the morning.

Lady Emma Brenham

"Hmmm...very interesting." He frowned, only then remembering the butler waited for his instructions. "You may go, Baxter. There is no need for any reply."

"Goodnight, my lord, Sir Edward." Baxter bowed himself from the room.

Edward settled himself in a nearby chair. "Some problem at your estate?"

Lucas looked up from his contemplation of the note. "No, no. This is from Lady Emma Brenham. Lady Dentley is her sister. I met them both today. It is pertaining to an unpleasant event that happened to Lady Emma at the Seating's ball tonight."

Edward sat up in his chair. "Lady Emma Brenham? Viscountess Dentley's sister…you can't mean *Bawdy Brenham*?"

He choked on his brandy. "What are you talking about?"

Edward stared at him. "Didn't you notice how well-endowed she is? Why, her breasts are so large they are often likened to beacons, barges, and barrels!"

He frowned at his friend. "I'll thank you not to repeat such hurtful things about her to me again. Even more importantly, never say anything about this if you happen to be in her company."

"Are you admonishing me? I mention this to you in the strictest confidence." Edward glared at him.

"I am sorry. I apologize for doubting you." He sighed, staring at the glowing embers in the fireplace before turning back to his friend. "I agree, Lady Emma is definitely built on Junoesque lines. She also has lovely warm, brown eyes."

"It appears I missed much by not being at the ball tonight," Edward replied with a cocked brow.

He set the note on a nearby table and got up to pour himself more brandy. "I need to understand something. Are you acquainted with a Sir Charles Walling?"

"That scoundrel?" Edward groaned. "He came within an inch of accusing me of cheating at a game of cards last month in London. I experienced a run of luck and he acted desperate. I believe he only stopped at calling me a cheat because I would call him out. He would face a person on the dueling field who is a much better shot than he is."

"I wouldn't be surprised. He attempted to force Lady Emma to agree to marry him by brutally accosting her tonight." Lucas took a sip of his drink.

"What?" Edward exclaimed. "He sounds half-baked as well as dishonest."

"I believe so." Lucas studied his glass. "There is no need to go into all the details, but I spotted him forcing himself on her on an outdoor balcony at the Seating house."

Edward gasped. "Inexcusable! I trust you planted the cad a facer?"

As he stared at his friend, the image of Sir Charles' face pressed to the ground with blood squirting from his nose brandished itself in front of his eyes. "Oh, yes, I made him suffer. I proceeded to escort him off the property and handed him into the care of a magistrate conveniently in the area, with the understanding he would leave Brighton immediately."

Edward finished his drink and got up to refill his glass. "Any idea why he treated her so savagely?"

Lucas picked up the note. "I sent Lady Emma a missive earlier tonight informing her I would make certain Sir Charles left the city. This is her answer. She believes the louse has serious money troubles and has probably fallen into the clutches of a money lender."

Edward took the piece of paper, studying it for a moment before handing it back to him. "After the reckless way he acted when I saw him last, I would say she is most certainly correct in her assumption."

He folded the note, placing it on the table. "I intend to join forces with her brother-in-law, Viscount Dentley tomorrow. It shouldn't take long to verify his location. But enough talk on this subject. Where were you this evening?"

Edward sighed before answering. "My mother and sister showed up on my doorstep just as my valet finished tying my cravat."

Lucas grimaced. "What? At your bachelor lodgings?"

Edward grinned. "Thankfully, I rented a three-bedroom house for the next two months. They are occupying the other two chambers."

"Are they planning on staying the entire summer?" He asked, as he stretched his legs out in front of him. "Such a state of affairs won't be very comfortable or convenient for you."

Edward drank the rest of the brandy in his glass. "Apparently my mother decided she wants to throw a summer house party on my estate next week. She and my sister made a detour here on their journey from London to convince me to join them."

He cocked a brow eyeing his friend in surprise. "At Horsham House? Do you intend to go?"

Edward met his gaze with a pained expression on his face. "My plans will definitely be upset. I looked forward to spending some time enjoying the seashore. I suppose it won't be too hard for my landlord to rent the house if I vacate it."

Lucas frowned. "You mother usually prefers to stay in London during the summer months. Why the sudden change?"

Edward snorted. "She claims she wants to invite some eligible gentlemen for my sister to meet in a more casual setting than what exists in London. Because my mother is insisting I join the party, I believe a few eligible ladies will be in attendance as well, intended for my perusal."

"I'm sorry you need to…wait a minute." Lucas stood up, placing his empty glass down on the table. "Would it be possible to include Lady Emma and myself as guests to this house party? Your home offers all kinds of possibilities for us to meet without the concern of risking her reputation. The conventional rules are considerably relaxed at such events. Your mother's presence lends more than enough respectability to the situation."

Edward came to his feet as well and slapped him on his back. "That's a capital idea! I believe Mother has an acquaintance with Lady Dentley. She could phrase the invitation in such a way to make it clear the party would be an opportunity for Lady Emma to meet other young people in an informal atmosphere. Do you hold a serious interest in the lady?"

He grinned at his friend. "She does intrigue me."

Edward laughed. "I don't mind admitting I prefer to have you in attendance if my mother should pressure me to make a choice from the group of the other ladies she is sure to invite. You could help me convince her I am not ready to take the plunge yet."

Lucas chuckled as he led him to the door. "As you are aware, I have plenty of experience dodging the *parson's mousetrap*. You can count on my assistance."

Chapter Nine

Shortly after Emma requested her note be delivered to Lord Millington, a knock sounded upon her bedchamber door. Mary answered the summons. A chamber maid stood outside in the hallway holding a small bowl covered by a white cloth.

The young girl walked inside the room and then bent over in an awkward, wobbly curtsey. "Lady Emma, Mrs. Moss sends you this compress with her compliments. You are to put it on top of the affected spot to relieve the soreness before you retire for the evening."

"Will you put it on my bedside table? Please give Mrs. Moss my sincere thanks...what is your name?"

The maid carefully placed the bowl on the table next to the bed. "It's Sally, my lady."

"Be sure to convey my gratitude to her, Sally."

"I will, my lady." The maid curtsied again and left the room.

Mary poured out her tea, adding the milk and sugar before placing the cup on the small table next to her bed. "Is there anything else you need at the moment, my lady? Do you need help with the compress?"

"No, thank you. I can manage. That will be all for tonight," she told her, anxious to be alone.

When the door closed behind her maid, she carried the missive Lord Millington sent across the room to her bed. She climbed in under the soft sheet and blankets, propping herself up on the pillows, to reread the note over several times. A warm tingle started in her belly working its way to her heart as the words...*I cannot be easy*...leaped out at her from the page. For some reason, the phrase written in his bold, masculine scrawl made her feel safe and secure.

She dropped the paper onto the table, took a sip of tea and then reached for a book about seasonal flowers in the Brighton area she located in the library downstairs. After several minutes of staring at the opening page without comprehending the words or pictures, she sighed and closed the book.

Her stomach muscles clenched painfully as a horrifying image appeared in front of her, Sir Charles, his eyes glazed, his mouth hanging open, drool rolling down his chin as he reached out to grasp her breast. She put a hand to her mouth as a wave of nausea rolled through her body. She tossed the blanket off her legs and ran to the chamber pot, bending over it as her belly heaved. As she hung over the bowl, she commanded herself to think of something else, soothing, calming thoughts. So much had occurred on this long, eventful day. A more desirable, exceptional form of Lord Millington soon presented itself. Minutes later, her body relaxed, and her breaths became more even. She wiped her face with a cloth and slowly made her way back to her bed to lie back against the pillows, staring up at the ceiling.

Recognizing him in the park as the gentleman who had assisted her in London, immediately after he saved her nephews from grave injury, started it all. She relived the intense pounding of her heart as she climbed the hill, terrified of what she would see when she reached the road. The rising hysteria was quickly replaced by fervent relief when she perceived the boys were unharmed. With Celia at her side, she learned his name and title. Lord Millington's quick action stopped almost certain disaster, the horrible idea of serious injury or even death to either of the boys was beyond comprehension. She shivered at the prospect of grief and heartache Celia and Vernon would experience if anything happened to their children. Emma wrapped her shawl more securely around her shoulders as she recalled only a few hours after ensuring her nephews' safety, she herself had been rescued by Lord Millington's timely intervention with Sir Charles. There certainly were many reasons to be grateful to him.

Not wishing to dwell once more on the horrifying circumstances pertaining to Sir Charles and his attack, Emma centered her thoughts on Lord Millington, his actions and their discussion after she arrived at the ball. He acted surprised by her interest in learning more about Mrs. Wilcox and her life in the United States. Obviously, he believed she lived with one purpose; to dress up and frequent the many balls and parties to be visited in London throughout most of the season. And then he made the cryptic comment about wanting to understand more about love and marriage.

But wait! She sat up against the pillows. Vernon mentioned Lord Millington's aversion to marriage earlier in the evening. How confusing!

Emma yawned, suddenly exhausted and ready to sleep. She took off her shawl and reached for Mrs. Moss' compress, securing it in place before extinguishing the candle and lying down in her bed.

****

Lucas rode up to the front of the Dentley estate early the following morning. He dismounted and handed the reins to a waiting groom. He strode across the graveled drive, swiftly mounting the front stairs. The door opened when he cleared the top step. The butler waited inside to take his hat, gloves, and riding crop.

The portly gentleman bowed. "Good morning. Lord Millington."

"Hello, Worth," he replied, remembering the butler's name from his hurried visit the evening before.

The butler handed his things to a waiting footman. "Lord Dentley will see you in his study."

"Thank you." He followed the man down the hallway.

Worth knocked on the last door.

"Come in."

"Lord Millington to see you, my lord." The butler bowed and left the room.

"Good morning, Lord Dentley." He closed the door behind him and walked up to the desk.

"Good morning. Let us disperse with formal titles. We will be working closely together. My first name is Vernon."

"Of course. My name is Lucas."

"Good. That is much easier." Vernon gestured to a nearby chair. "Take a seat. Is there any more information pertaining to Sir Charles and his whereabouts today?"

He sat down. "I received a note from Lady Emma last night informing me of her theory for his rash actions last evening. Has she spoken to you this morning?"

Vernon sat up straighter in his chair and raised his eyebrows. "No, she isn't down yet. What did she relate to you?"

He cleared his throat before speaking. "She believes Sir Charles is experiencing a shortage of funds. His desperate actions last night might possibly be blamed on a visit to a money lender in London and a demand for immediate payment. She also thinks he made plans to marry a wealthy merchant's daughter, but for some reason this event did not take place."

Vernon cupped his chin with his hand, staring down at his desk. "Very interesting. While it in no way excuses his attack on Emma, it certainly could cause Sir Charles to panic, to act irrationally."

Lucas rubbed his hands together, studying the glowing coal in the fireplace. "Yes, I certainly agree."

"We should be on our way as soon as possible." Vernon glanced at him. "Did you ride over?"

"Yes, I brought my stallion."

Vernon rose from his chair. "Give me a moment. I need to speak to Worth."

Lucas stood up and walked across the room to stare out a nearby window at the garden below while his companion flung the study door open. "Worth, will you request my horse be brought around as quickly as possible? Oh, Emma, there you are! Come in. How are you feeling this morning? I planned to inquire if you were downstairs."

"Good morning, Vernon. I feel much better, thank you," she replied in a subdued tone.

Lucas turned around, swiftly taking in her appearance from his vantage point as she walked into the room. She wore a lavender morning gown that brought out the deep brown color of her hair and enhanced her lush figure. She looked lovely and well-rested.

"Hello, Lady Emma. I'm very happy to hear you are

better this morning. You look enchanting." He bowed to her.

She whirled around and stared at him, blushing as she put a hand over her chest. "I...I am extremely glad to see you, my lord. I...I planned to tell my brother-in-law of my ideas on the possible reason for Sir Charles' rash actions. I trust you received my note last night?"

"The gown is beautiful on you. Any adjustment would harm the effect," he assured her, smiling in a carefree, reassuring manner. "I got your missive. Vernon and I were just discussing it."

"We both believe you are onto something important." Vernon bent over to gather a few papers from his desk. "After we make certain Sir Charles isn't in Brighton, we will go to London to see if we can obtain information about his spending habits or of any recent loans from moneylenders."

"Pardon me, Lord Millington, I want to ask a question." Lady Emma looked directly at him, speaking through trembling lips. "Where...Where did you tell Sir Charles to go last night?"

"I dragged him out of a side door into the street where I observed the local magistrate questioning a couple of lads," Lucas appraised her. "Without mentioning your name, I told the gentleman, a Mr. White, Sir Charles assaulted a lady and requested he be escorted away from the city without delay."

She walked toward the chair Lucas recently vacated, clutching the back of it with one hand. "Did he make any comment during your discussion with the magistrate? I find it hard to believe he wouldn't argue or put up a fight when faced with the prospect of being forced to leave Brighton."

"He made a threatening remark about having influence in high places," he admitted to her. "He accompanied the magistrate without further complaint. At that point, I rushed inside to check on you."

She sighed and then offered a hesitant smile directed at himself and her brother-in-law. "I am grateful to both of you for going on this journey to discover Sir Charles' location. I admit I will be uneasy until I know he left the city."

Lucas walked up to stand next to her. "We will not rest until we gain the information we require."

Vernon stood at her other side. "We will make certain there is no further cause for concern about any repetition of Sir Charles' cruel, savage behavior. Now if you both will excuse me, I must say good-bye to my wife and children."

The door clicked shut behind him leaving them alone inside the room. Lucas reached for her hand, placing on his arm before commenting, "I wonder if your brother-in-law is attempting to test my restraint. Let's go out into the foyer."

"What are you referring to? Oh, yes; I had forgotten your reputation."

He frowned at her, his turn to be perplexed. "My hesitation to be alone with you has nothing at all to do with my reputed actions with other women in my past. I am attracted to you and certainly wish to become better acquainted. However, those concerns need to be pushed aside for the moment. It is of utmost importance we ensure your safety before anything else can be resolved."

"I'm…I'm sorry. I am overset. I spoke rashly." She turned her head away from him, gripping his sleeve as he guided her out of the room.

As they crossed the threshold he bent over to whisper in her ear. A strand of a wayward piece of her silky hair tickled his nose. "Apology accepted."

They stopped in the hallway, not speaking, gazing into each other's eyes.

"Your horse is ready, my lord." Worth's low-toned comment broke through their reverie.

"Oh!" She staggered backward a step. "Keep safe on the journey."

"You take care as well. Good-bye." He gently removed her hand from his arm, turning away as the butler handed him his gloves, hat, and riding crop. He made his way to the entry and out the door, striding down the front steps without looking back. He walked up to his horse, taking the reins from the groom just as Lord Dentley's animal came around the corner of the drive, being led by another servant.

Moments later, Vernon joined him and commented, "I'm thinking we should start with a visit to Mr. White and then head to Lord Parker's home."

Lucas swung his leg over his horse, settling himself in the saddle. "My thought as well. Even if the magistrate can assure us he left the area, Sir Charles would find some way to notify his sister of his plans. He couldn't risk the chance she might become concerned for his safety and call the watch on him."

"Possibly Lord Parker can provide us with more information on the state of Sir Charles' finances." Vernon mounted his horse.

"That would be extremely useful," he agreed. "I contacted the magistrate this morning. He has consented to meet us at The Bedford Tavern."

The two men guided their houses toward the center

of town and soon arrived in front of the pub. After tossing some coins to a couple of enterprising boys who volunteered to hold their animals for them while they were gone, Lucas and Vernon made their way inside the building.

Lucas quickly spotted Mr. White seated at the bar nursing a pint. A pock-marked woman wearing a rumpled, low-cut dress barely covering her nipples hovered nearby. He indicated he would take the corner booth after catching the magistrate's attention. They walked over to the table and sat down.

Lucas ordered a couple of pints of ale from the woman before the man ambled across the room to join them.

"Good day to you, my lord. You wished to speak to me?" He wedged his bulky frame into a chair.

"I did. This is Viscount Dentley. We want to make certain the person I ordered you to take away last night actually left the city." He stared unflinchingly at the magistrate as the servant placed their pints on the table.

Mr. White's face turned dark red, and he hesitated before speaking, "Uh, I handed him over to his brother-in-law, Lord Parker, your lordships. He assured me he would see Sir Charles left the city this morning."

Lucas paused with his glass halfway to his mouth. He slowly lowered the tankard back down to the table with an unsteady hand, glaring at the man. "Are you telling me the blackguard spent the night in Brighton and most probably is still here?"

"Speak up, man. Where is Sir Charles? Did you not understand this man assaulted a lady last evening?" Vernon questioned in a shaking voice.

A bead of perspiration rolled down the magistrate's

forehead. He wiped it away with a dirt-smudged handkerchief. "Lord Parker promised me he would be gone at first light."

Lucas stood up, tossing some coins onto the wooden table. Vernon came to his feet and headed out the door.

"I'll not make a scene because a lady is involved," Lucas spoke in a harsh whisper to the magistrate. "If I were you, I would hope Sir Charles has truly gone because if he is still in the area, he will most likely attempt to kidnap the woman in question."

"No! Never say so!" the man blurted out as Lucas turned away without further comment and rushed outside.

Vernon mounted his horse. Lucas quickly followed suit. Without speaking, they turned their animals around in the street and cantered in the direction of the Parker residence.

A few minutes later, they were each tossing their reins to a waiting groom in front of the house. Vernon reached the door first pounding his fist against the smooth surface.

The door swung wide. A flustered butler appeared in the opening. "What…what is the meaning of this?"

Lucas stepped around Vernon. "Lord Dentley and Lord Millington. We are here to see your master on a matter of grave importance. Take us to him immediately."

The butler's agitated visage turned to one of apprehension. "Of course, my lords. Right this way."

They followed on the heels of the discomposed butler. He led them down a long hallway decorated at intervals by marble statues of men and women in various stages of undress. He stopped in front of a large wooden door and knocked.

"Come."

"Lord Dentley and Lord Millington to see you, my lord." The butler made the perfunctory announcement before turning away, disappearing down the hall.

Lucas and Vernon strode into the room, slamming the door behind them.

"To what do I owe this visit from two such illustrious gentlemen?" A balding, middle-aged man with a portly middle struggled to stand up from behind a desk.

"We are here to take your brother-in-law off your hands." Vernon spoke in a savage tone.

Lord Parker raised his bushy eyebrows and glared at him. "Sir Charles left at dawn. He is on his way to London."

Lucas strode forward, slamming his palm on the desktop. "You cannot be unaware of what took place last night. What makes you so certain he is headed there? We believe he intends to remain in Brighton unless he is forcefully turned out of the city."

Lord Parker cleared his throat. "He is going there because I provided him with funds to appease his creditors and a partial payment on a large gambling debt. If you wish to verify the information, I will give you the particulars, names, amounts and so forth. He needs to get the money to them before they call out their thugs and proceed to break every bone in his body."

"Why did you give that louse anything?" Vernon muttered through tightened lips.

Lord Parker gave them each a cold stare before answering, "To calm my wife and get the good-for-nothing knave out of my house. I trust you can sympathize with my reasons?"

Lucas turned away, striding to the door, and yanking it open. Vernon remained near the desk, presumably determined to collect the details Lord Parker alluded to. He needed to leave the premises at once. His right hand was balled into a fist; any moment he would plant the man a facer. He couldn't refrain from making one last observation. "I can only hope Sir Charles falls from his horse and breaks his neck on the journey, certainly a much more satisfying conclusion."

Chapter Ten

Emma felt thrilling, tingly warmth rippling throughout her body from the top of her head to the tip of her toes in reaction to Lord Millington's intimate gesture, unlike anything she ever experienced before. His lips brushed the tip of her earlobe when he whispered into her ear. Something stirred deep in her soul as she stared into his radiant blue eyes moments later. She stood in the entry studying him as he walked away from her, willing herself to never forget the marvelous sensation before she lost sight of him as he went out the front door. When Vernon and Celia joined her a few minutes later, she remained bemused in a sentimental, emotional haze.

Celia put her hand on her arm as she watched her husband descend the stairs. "Vernon will take care of this troubling, appalling matter, Emma. Do not be concerned. I will miss him while he is away."

"I believe Lord Millington will strive to learn the answers we require as quickly as possible," she countered, still engrossed in a sensual reverie.

Her sister turned to her with her eyebrows raised. "Well, that is certainly a comforting image. I am happy to hear you hold him in such high regard. Shall we see what Cook has prepared for us this morning? We will need the energy. I'm certain we will be beset by many visitors today."

A little over an hour later, they were both in the

sitting room ready to receive callers. They had just seated themselves when Worth came to the door to announce Lady Parker and her daughter.

The lady burst into the room, followed closely by Annabelle, who kept her gaze trained on the floor, barely acknowledging them. They sat on a nearby settee.

"I wanted to come to inquire as to the state of your health, Lady Emma," Lady Parker came straight to the point, wasting no time on niceties.

"Thankfully, I am much improved," she spoke the words in a terse, imperious manner.

"I am greatly relieved to hear that," the lady rushed on. "I wished to inform you my brother spoke to me briefly late last night. He maintains a misunderstanding occurred at the ball. He means to discuss the incident with you and explain himself."

As the aggravating woman's words echoed in her ears, Emma's heart raced painfully inside her chest. She choked, suddenly struggling to breathe. Her hands, only moments before folded together and relaxed on her lap, now shook with trepidation. It sounded as if Sir Charles had stayed in Brighton. She never wanted to see him again. She took a deep breath, forcing out words. "You…you alarm me. This cannot be true. I understand a magistrate escorted your brother away from the ball yesterday evening. He…He left the city directly. I also disagree with something else you stated. Your…Your brother's intentions were perfectly clear. He tried to force me to marry him against my wishes."

Lady Parker made a snorting noise. She studied Emma in a bold manner before speaking. "Charles would never hurt you. You are obviously top heavy in the bosom. Are you certain you didn't lose your balance, and bump the balustrade?"

Celia gasped. Emma stood up, glaring down at the foolish, cruel-hearted woman. "Your brother forced himself on me. I have absolutely no confusion as to his intent. If you require confirmation, I suggest you speak with Lord Millington. Thank goodness he arrived when he did. He can vouch for the fact I am not exaggerating."

Lady Parker ignored her words. "You were fond of Charles. You need to marry him."

Emma clutched her shaking hands together while fuming inside. "Listen to me very carefully. I don't wish to say this again. I will never, ever marry Sir Charles Walling."

Celia cleared her throat as she came to her feet. "I believe I must ask you and your daughter to leave at once, Lady Parker. My sister suffered greatly last night. There is no call for her to be hurt again today by your evil, deceptive comments."

Lady Parker sputtered and reached out to grip the arm of the settee as she struggled to rise from her seat. "Very well, Lady Dentley. I will take my leave if you insist. But I fail to see how I caused Lady Emma agony. I am simply pleading my brother's case. Come, Annabelle."

As her mother strode through the door, Annabelle moved to stand beside Emma. She whispered, "Uncle Charles is desperate."

"What do you mean?" she asked.

Annabelle's eyes glistened with unshed tears. "I couldn't sleep. I heard them talking last night. Uncle Charles needs money badly. He gambled away everything. My father gave him some last night, but he said he needs more."

"Annabelle, come here!" ordered Lady Parker.

"I must go." She turned and rushed from the room.

Emma and Celia stared at each other in silence until the sound of the receding footsteps of the two women had faded away. Emma waited to speak until she heard Worth close the front door behind them. "Did you hear what Annabelle said?"

"Yes, I did." Her sister frowned.

Emma pondered the girl's words. "It appears my hunch about Sir Charles is correct."

"He is definitely desperate for money, but it is so hard for me to understand why he believed brutal force would make you accept him," Celia replied, lifting one shaking hand to her forehead.

"Obviously, he is out of time. He couldn't afford to waste days or weeks visiting the *marriage mart* to look around for another heiress. He counted on our past casual friendship to make me open to his proposal. But he couldn't woo me in the conventional manner. He most certainly requires the funds immediately." Emma sighed and walked across the room to a window to study a pink rose bush in the garden outside. "I wish I could tell Vernon and Lord Millington the information we learned today."

Worth stepped inside the room and bowed. "The Countess of Watford is here to see you, Lady Emma."

Emma turned to her sister. "Lord Millington's mother. I met her briefly last night. Why should she visit me?"

Celia's eyebrows rose and she shrugged her shoulders. "We shall find out. Show her in, Worth."

The diminutive older lady Emma vaguely remembered from the previous evening strode into the room. Today, tucked under a bonnet of dark blue satin, her abundant silver tresses shone. The brim of the hat was trimmed with a band of blue and white plaid material. She wore a round gown of light blue muslin, topped by a spencer in a slightly darker shade, richly ornamented with white satin. Half boots covered her small feet. She nodded her head regally to Celia and then to Emma before speaking. "I missed the opportunity to further our acquaintance at the ball, Lady Emma. Unfortunately, my time is extremely limited this morning."

Emma curtsied to her and turned to Celia. "I don't believe you met my sister, Lady Dentley."

Celia curtsied as well. "I am happy to make your acquaintance, Lady Watford. Please sit down."

"Thank you." Lady Watford settled herself on a nearby chair. She sat rigid and upright with her chin thrust outward. "Lady Dentley, it has come to my attention my son unexpectedly returned to London early this morning in the company of your husband."

"I…" Celia looked over at Emma in confusion.

She quickly took control of the conversation. "Lady Watford, your son is assisting my brother-in-law in a personal matter."

The countess raised her eyebrows, opening her eyes wide to glare at her. "Indeed? Am I not to be told what this concern is?"

Emma cleared her throat before answering. "Lord Millington will apprise you of what he deems appropriate to divulge when he returns."

Lady Watford grunted. "Can you tell me when that will be?"

"My husband expects to return late tomorrow, at the

latest the following morning," Celia informed her.

"I am extremely displeased to hear this, Lady Dentley." The countess frowned at her. "My son has important obligations to fulfill today. Influential members of our social circle will be offended if he is not present."

"Please explain to the affected parties the issue is urgent. Surely they will understand?" Emma inquired.

Lady Watford huffed with obvious annoyance. "I see I must be frank with you, or I will get nowhere. My son is engaged to spend the afternoon with the woman he intends to marry."

Emma knew a painful, squeezing sensation in the region of her heart. She took a ragged breath before speaking. "Per…perhaps he sent a note before he left and explained the matter to her?"

"No, he did not. I have just come from Lord and Lady Breech's home. Lady Sophia received nothing from him," the countess countered, in a resolute tone.

Emma gulped. "Lady Sophia?"

Lady Watford scowled at her. "Yes. Lady Sophia Hampton, daughter of Lord and Lady Breech. You were introduced last night."

Emma gasped as she recalled the beautiful woman with the thick black hair and unusual violet eyes. "She…she is Lord Millington's betrothed?"

The countess looked away toward the window on the other side of the room before replying in a gruff manner. "No, not officially, but a formal announcement is imminent."

"I'm very sorry such an important obligation will be missed," Celia stated, with sincerity. "We will be certain to inform Lord Millington of your visit when my husband and he return."

Lady Watford didn't answer for a moment. She faced them, her gaze concentrating on Emma. "My son exhibited a curious preoccupation with your presence last night. Does this urgent matter that made him forget important engagements and take him away to London, relate to you, Lady Emma?"

"I…"

Thankfully, Worth appeared at the door and bowed. "Lady Seating is here to see you, my lady."

Celia stood and pointedly glanced at Emma before replying to the butler. "Ask her to wait a moment, Worth."

Lady Watford came to her feet and walked to the still-open door. "I can sense it is pointless to stay here and expect you to provide me with additional information. I must take my leave and disclose what little I learned about my son's whereabouts to the others. Good day."

Emma rose from her seat to watch in silence as the countess strode down the long hallway and disappear out the front entry. Then she walked across the carpeted floor to the window to resume her study of the garden.

"I noticed you were as surprised as I to hear of Lord Millington's attraction to this Lady Sophia," Celia commented.

"Yes, it is astonishing," she murmured.

Lady Seating bustled into the room. "I came as soon as I could, Lady Dentley. I wished to inquire as to the state of Lady Emma's health."

"Thank you. She is much better. You can see for yourself." Celia pointed to Emma standing in the far corner of the room.

"I never dreamed you would rise from your bed this day!" Lady Seating exclaimed, as she pulled a lace handkerchief from her reticule and mopped her brow.

Emma walked toward her, taking several deep breaths to calm herself. It would never do to give any hints of the anger and anxiety she experienced as a result of the previous guests' visits before this babbling, gossipy woman. "I am doing well, thank you for inquiring. My sister's housekeeper has a great talent for making cold compresses to relieve soreness and swelling. I woke this morning with almost no ill effects from my ordeal last night."

Lady Seating waved her handkerchief across her chest in a distracted manner. "I am very relieved to hear you say that. Such an unfortunate incident to occur at my ball!"

"I trust your other guests were not aware anything untoward took place?" Emma questioned her, in a compelling tone.

"No, thank goodness." Lady Seating wiped her brow once again before tucking her handkerchief away in her reticule. "Some people commented on Lady Parker's early departure but none of the other guests were aware of Sir Charles' presence."

"That is certainly a great comfort to us," Celia replied. "Will you sit down?"

"No, no, Lady Dentley, I cannot stay," she answered, with a hurried stream of words. "I wished only to offer you my greetings and to check on your sister's health. I am deeply sorry about Sir Charles' actions last evening. I hope he never bothers you again, Lady Emma."

Even though she couldn't be certain the reprobate

had actually left town, Emma believed it would be prudent not to involve Lady Seating any further. "Thank you. My brother-in-law and Lord Millington are even now tracing Sir Charles' location so I may rest easy with the knowledge he is no longer in the city. I am certain neither he nor his sister will ever speak of what happened at your party; his beastly behavior would be condemned in society."

"It is great comfort to hear those two fine gentlemen are checking his trail," Lady Seating agreed as she gathered her shawl around her shoulders. "I must be off. I need to make four more calls before I can return home and put my feet up."

After she left, Emma took a deep breath and faced her sister. "Do you mind if I go out and sit in the garden for a while? I am suddenly feeling very tired."

Celia looked concerned. "Of course, you shouldn't do too much today. I can certainly entertain anyone else who should happen to call."

Emma managed a feeble smile. "Thank you. The warm sunshine will quickly set me to rights. You comprehend how partial I am to spending time in my own garden."

"I suppose it would be a waste of time to ask you to wear a hat?"

"You are correct, Celia."

Chapter Eleven

Lucas vaulted up the front steps on the heels of Viscount Dentley. The door to the estate swung open as they crossed the landing.

"Worth, we need to speak to Emma without delay. Where is she?" Vernon inquired of his butler.

"Lady Emma is in the garden, my lord."

Lucas wrestled with the sensation of panic threatening to engulf him as he heard the man's words. "Is she alone?"

"I believe so, my lord."

"What is the fastest way there, through the house?" He willed himself to remain outwardly calm.

"There is a gate around the side." Vernon spoke the sentence in a terse, anxious manner.

Both men charged back down the steps, walking briskly to the garden. Lucas became conscious of the sound of his heart pounding loudly in his ears. What if Sir Charles did not leave for London? Did he wait for a chance to find Lady Emma alone, capture her and take her away? He told himself to relax and not jump to any conclusions. He studied the grassy area, spotting a bright splash of pink from a cluster of roses behind a fence. He noted the sweet calls of several birds in the trees overhead. It was a reassuring sound; no cries of alarm reached his ears.

"She usually sits back there." Vernon pointed

toward the rose bushes as he reached to unlatch the gate. "Emma, where are you?"

"I'm over here."

"Thank goodness," Lucas muttered, taking a few deep breaths. He followed Vernon as he made his way down a pathway bordering the grassy area. The sound of Emma's lovely voice brought a heady sense of relief and his heart slowed to its normal pace. He spotted her sitting on a stone bench at the rear of the garden, with a thick shawl wrapped around her shoulders.

She came to her feet as they approached. "Vernon, Lord Millington, is something wrong?"

Her brother-in-law gave her a quick hug. Lucas clutched the hand she offered him.

"We apologize for confronting you in our travel dirt. We wanted to pass on what we learned this morning to you without delay," Lucas told her, with a relieved sigh.

"There…there is much to relay to you," panted Vernon.

She studied them both. "I'm eager to hear what you uncovered. Why are you both acting as if you ran for miles to get here?"

"We were concerned for your safety when we learned you were in the garden on your own," Vernon admitted, echoing Lucas' silent worry moments before.

"As you can see, I'm perfectly fine…" She frowned as the significance of her brother-in-law's words sank in. She slowly lowered herself back down onto the bench. "I imagine you are going to inform me why I should be anxious about my safety. There is something of importance to tell you both as well."

"I expect you are tired after last night's ordeal," Vernon spoke in a soothing tone. "We will make this as brief as possible."

"I admit I experienced some weariness after spending the day inside, but the fresh air has revived me. I feel much better."

"I'm very happy to hear that," Lucas replied with a smile. He turned to Vernon. "Should I start?"

"Go ahead."

He cleared his throat. "First, we met the magistrate in town who I relinquished Sir Charles to last night. After asking Mr. White to verify he left, he admitted instead of escorting Sir Charles from the city as I demanded, he released him to the custody of Lord Parker."

She cast a furtive glance at the shrubbery bordering the garden. "Are you saying he never left the city?"

"Don't panic, Emma," Vernon interjected. "The magistrate also informed us that Lord Parker promised him Sir Charles would be gone by first light this morning."

"What did you learn?"

Vernon sat down next to her. "Lord Millington and I paid a visit to the Parker estate as soon as we heard Sir Charles did not leave last night. We confronted Lord Parker and were able to discover he gave into his brother-in-law's pleas for money."

Lucas propped one booted foot on a protruding rock next to the bench. "To be specific, Lord Parker provided Sir Charles with two drafts totaling seven thousand pounds. One draft is for two thousand pounds. It is apparently a partial payment of some vowels held by a Lord John Putney from a recent gaming loss. The other draft for the remaining five thousand pounds is to serve as an installment on the funds borrowed by Sir Charles."

Vernon reached over to squeeze her hand. "Lord

Millington refers to the money loaned to him by a Mr. Topper Sloan, a notorious London *ten percenter*. Lord Parker did not divulge the total amount Sir Charles has squandered."

Emma gasped, covering her mouth with her free hand. "Lady Parker paid a visit today. She brought her daughter as well. Just before she left, Annabelle managed to whisper to me she heard a discussion between her parents and Sir Charles last night. She verified he is indeed in desperate circumstances. How could he believe my modest inheritance would cover the amount he requires to come about again?"

Lucas frowned at the ground as he considered her query. "People like him who develop gambling fever believe redemption is always just around the corner. He probably thought his luck would turn and he would start winning, once he fobbed off the money lender with what became his property when you married him."

Vernon frowned at Emma. "Did Lady Parker say something to upset you?"

She turned to him. "Yes, she made me very uneasy when I understood her brother visited them last evening. She claimed he told her a *misunderstanding* took place. He is determined to speak with me again."

Vernon released her hand and came to his feet. "We intend to be able to assure you tomorrow or perhaps the morning after, the only thing Sir Charles is concerned with at this time is getting the drafts his brother-in-law provided him with back to the appropriate people in London. Lord Millington and I are going to obtain rooms at an inn tonight near Croydon. Tomorrow we take an easy ride into the city. We will arrive early to make certain Sir Charles is there, with no intention of returning to Brighton."

She sighed. "You give me comfort with those words."

Vernon helped her rise from the bench. "We must be off. There is a great deal of riding to do."

She hugged him. "Goodbye. I wish you both a safe journey."

"I will pack a bag and take my leave of Celia." Vernon turned away, striding toward the house.

Lucas bent over a nearby rose bush to snap off a tender bud with yellow petals. He handed it to her with a flourish, bowing at the waist. "Until later, then."

She blushed and held the flower to her nose for a moment. "Thank you. There...There is something I must tell you before you go. Your mother visited me today. She somehow perceived you left Brighton early this morning in the company of my brother-in-law. She wished to be told of your whereabouts."

He swore under his breath. "What did you tell her?"

"I said you assisted Vernon with a personal matter. You would divulge the information you deemed appropriate to her when you returned."

He scowled as an image of his mother's probable reaction to such an evasive answer played out in his head. "Did that satisfy her?"

She looked directly at him, thrusting out her chin before answering. "She is quite upset. Apparently, a previous engagement existed to spend the afternoon with your *intended*."

He started in surprise, staring at her with brows raised. "My what?"

She pursed her full lips, grimacing. "You heard me. Your intended. I have no confusion as to her meaning.

She also said the betrothal is not official, and an announcement is imminent."

"Botheration! Will they never cease their meddling?" He turned away to compose himself before confronting her again. "It is not an appropriate time to speak of this matter, but let me say she is wrong, completely mistaken."

"It has nothing to do with me, my lord," she disputed. "I simply wished to forewarn you of Lady Watford's comments before she confronts you about the missed engagement."

He grimaced at his mother's obvious attempt to put Lady Emma in an uncomfortable position. "Thank you. I will explain later."

She frowned at him. "I certainly do not require any clarification."

"I will offer my apologies for my mother's insensitive comments, then. Goodbye." He turned away, trembling with rage and frustration. He squeezed his fingers tightly together against the skin of his palms until he drew blood.

****

Emma wandered around the garden for several minutes, clutching the rose in her hand as she deliberated the predicament involving Lord Millington. There were many reasons to be grateful to him in the short amount of time that had passed since their unplanned introduction. Because of his heroic actions, she deliberately ignored Vernon's words describing his reputation to her before the Seating's ball. She talked herself into believing he could be nothing other than an honorable, forthright gentleman. After hearing Lady Watford's implications, it appeared he acted as any other rake, amusing himself before he settled down and married. She idly strolled up the back steps and walked into the house. She paused when she saw Celia hurrying toward her. "What is wrong?"

"Just as Vernon and Lord Millington were leaving, Mrs. Wilcox arrived. She is asking for you. Whatever is the matter?"

Emma stood stock-still with her hand pressed to her forehead. "I accompanied Mrs. Wilcox to the ladies' retiring room last night after we sampled the food at the buffet. While I waited for her, Sir Charles confronted me, pulled me down the hallway and out onto the balcony. Of course, I never returned. With everything that occurred, I forgot all about Mrs. Wilcox. She must wonder what became of me."

Celia looked worried. "Do you wish to speak to her alone? I can continue to deal with other callers."

Emma gave her a relieved smile. "Yes, I would appreciate that."

"I instructed Worth take her to the morning room. I'll see that you're not disturbed."

She gave Celia a quick kiss on the cheek, handing her the flower. "Thank you. Will you put this in some water?"

She strode down the hallway to find Worth standing at the door with his hand upon the knob. "Lady Emma to see you, Mrs. Wilcox," he announced as he bowed her into the room.

She rushed forward to clasp Mrs. Wilcox's outstretched hands as she slowly came to her feet from her seat by the fireplace. "I'm so sorry. I caused you great worry last evening."

Mrs. Wilcox gently squeezed her fingers while she

intently studied her face. "I bumped into Lord Millington in the hallway not long after I began to search for you. He assured me you were safe but would leave the ball as soon as possible."

"I am extremely glad he put you at ease. Please sit down." She took a seat opposite her. "There is much to tell you."

The older lady lowered herself into the overstuffed chair once again giving her a frank, direct look. "I am ready to listen. I admit I am very curious as to what occurred last night."

"Would you like me to ring for some tea?"

"No, no. I am fine, my dear."

Emma settled back in her chair. "So much has happened since I saw you last. Where shall I begin?"

Mrs. Wilcox studied her for a moment before she spoke. "Tell me the parts you think I should be aware of. If you require my opinion or my ideas on anything at all, I promise I'll give you an honest answer."

After those reassuring comments, she cleared her throat before speaking. "Soon after we parted last night, I heard my name called in a frantic manner. I turned around to see an acquaintance of mine from London, Sir Charles Walling, standing close to me in the hallway. Sir Charles is Lady Parker's brother."

Mrs. Wilcox stared fixedly at her and edged forward on her chair. "Lady Parker mentioned her brother when we were speaking together in the buffet room. She said he looked forward to seeing you again."

"Oh, yes, you are right," she agreed, with a scowl. "It slipped my mind. I had no wish to renew my association with him, as I am sure you observed when I spoke with Lady Parker. Little did I comprehend how right I could be to feel hesitant about meeting Sir Charles again under any conditions."

Mrs. Wilcox didn't speak as she made this startling pronouncement.

Emma paused to collect herself and then continued. "He insisted he needed to speak to me in private. When I refused, he forced me to accompany him outside on a deserted balcony."

"You alarm me." Mrs. Wilcox frowned. "I should have insisted you wait for me inside the retiring room."

She attempted a reassuring smile. "We could not be aware Sir Charles would suddenly make an appearance or act in such a frantic, crazed manner."

"I suppose not." Mrs. Wilcox looked intently at her. "Were you hurt?"

Emma closed her eyes as she relived the terrifying moments that followed once Sir Charles trapped her on the balcony. She opened them again to find Mrs. Wilcox staring at her with some concern. "He accosted me. Thankfully, Lord Millington arrived on the scene moments later."

Mrs. Wilcox gasped as Emma continued to describe Sir Charles' hurtful actions. "I am so sorry to hear of this. I trust Lord Millington fought him off. You are not severely injured?"

"Lord Millington came to my rescue," Emma affirmed and then grimaced, putting a hand over her chest. "I experienced some bruising. My sister's housekeeper provided assistance. She is an authority on cold compresses; she gets much practice on my rambunctious nephews, tending to their cuts and bruises. There is just a bit of soreness left today."

Mrs. Wilcox gripped the top of her cane, rapping it

against the hardwood floor in obvious agitation. "Lady Parker's brother needs a sound thrashing. I hope Lord Millington dealt with the deranged man accordingly?"

Emma reached for her handkerchief, clutching it in her lap. She took a deep breath before answering. "My brother-in-law and Lord Millington are attempting to learn his exact location. They believe he returned to London. They will hopefully verify this in person tomorrow. Meanwhile, Lady Parker visited me today claiming her brother feels what happened at the ball can be easily explained as a misunderstanding. He told her he intends to confront me soon."

Mrs. Wilcox's eyes widened. "The colossal nerve of the man! How could he believe you wanted anything further to do with him?"

"I...I never want to see him again!" She sobbed, gripping her handkerchief. "I am most anxious to hear he definitely left the city of Brighton."

"Oh, Emma! I am so sorry this happened. You won't rest easy until you comprehend he has truly gone." Mrs. Wilcox stood up, leaning on her cane. "You are upset, my dear, understandably so. I will go."

She came to her feet, facing the older lady. "I...I want to apologize again for causing you to worry last night."

Mrs. Wilcox patted her arm before she made her way across the room. She paused at the door to turn and say, "I am so grateful Lord Millington happened by and came to your assistance. Goodbye, my dear."

"So am I. So am I," Emma whispered to herself, as she watched her friend walk down the hallway.

Chapter Twelve

"I am going to stop and pick up some sweets for my wife. You go on ahead and tell Emma our news."

Lucas nodded his agreement as Vernon turned his horse toward the main shops in town. He glanced up at the dusky, azure blue sky as he guided his stallion toward the Dentley estate. They had made good time on their journey back from London.

Minutes later, he rode up the driveway to the front of the property. When he reached the house, he got off his horse, handing the reins to a waiting groom. "Rub him down thoroughly. Give him some food and water. He has worked hard today."

"Yes, my lord."

He turned, swiftly mounting the front steps. The door opened before he reached the top stair.

"Good afternoon, my lord."

"Hello, Worth. Is Lady Emma available to see me?"

"I believe she is in her bedchamber getting ready for the evening meal. Lady Dentley is already in the drawing room. Would you care to join her? I will inform Lady Emma's maid you are here."

"Thank you." He followed the butler down the hallway.

"Lord Millington is here to see Lady Emma, my lady," Worth announced from the door.

"Oh, please show him in," Lady Dentley answered.

He strode through the open door and bowed. "I came as soon as I could. I wanted to apprise your sister of what we were able to learn."

Lady Dentley stood up from her chair near the fireplace. She wore a pale pink evening gown with a matching overskirt shot with silver threads and decorated with small white roses on the edge of her cap sleeves. "Good afternoon, Lord Millington. Is my husband not with you?"

"No, I'm sorry. He stopped in town to buy you a gift." The situation proved awkward. He silently berated himself for his rush to see Lady Emma. It made more sense to arrive in Lord Dentley's company.

"How sweet of him," Lady Dentley remarked, not appearing concerned by her husband's delay. "My sister will be down momentarily."

The door opened behind him. Lady Emma stood on the threshold.

"Hello, Lord Millington."

He opened his mouth to answer her greeting but shut it again, at a loss for words. She wore a Pomona green evening gown. It clung to her generous curves. The color served to emphasize the deep brown of her eyes. Her thick auburn hair was swept up into a loose coil on the crown of her head, allowing stray tendrils to caress her neck. Leaving the door ajar, she stepped forward into the room a few steps and then stopped. "Where is Vernon?"

"Lord Millington informed me he stopped in town to purchase a gift for me," Lady Dentley told her. "He does spoil me so."

"Oh. Yes, he certainly does." Lady Emma turned back to him. "Is there news of Sir Charles?"

He cleared his throat before replying. "Your

brother-in-law and I came upon him leaving Lord Putney's townhouse in London. He was visibly shocked to see us, and we were hopeful he would cooperate with us. But after he recovered from his surprise, he lapsed into his surly, churlish manner again."

"Did you manage to obtain his promise to stay away from me and from Brighton?" Lady Emma clenched her hands together at the front of her gown, staring at him intently.

"Why don't we all sit down?" Lady Dentley motioned him to a nearby chair. She indicated a place on the settee nearby for her sister to occupy.

They settled themselves before he spoke again. "We spent some time reasoning and arguing with him. Eventually Sir Charles reluctantly agreed to write a note promising he would stay out of the city. We followed him to his temporary lodgings in London where he penned the missive and handed it over to your brother-in-law. I haven't read it."

A commotion sounded at the door. He turned to see Vernon enter the room.

"I am sorry I'm late, but I wanted to purchase this for you." He strode up to his wife, handing her a gaily wrapped box before clasping her in his arms.

Lady Dentley clutched the gift in one hand while she returned her husband's embrace. "Thank you so much, my dear."

"You are welcome. Enjoy them." He gave her a kiss on her cheek before releasing her and turning to Lady Emma. He placed his hands on her shoulders. "How are you feeling?"

"I am much better," she assured him. "Lord Millington just informed us you located Sir Charles and he has agreed to stay away from me. Apparently, you are holding a note from him as well. I am curious to learn what he wrote."

"Yes, it is here." Vernon stepped away, reaching into his coat pocket. He pulled out a crumpled piece of parchment and sat down next to Lady Emma. "Stand behind us so you can read it as well, Lucas."

He took a place on the other side of the settee, raising his brows with dismay as he glimpsed dark blots of black ink and crossed words covering the note as Lord Dentley unfolded the paper. "Besides requiring stringent lessons in how a gentleman should treat a lady, the man certainly needs some instruction in the art of fine penmanship!"

"Here, Emma." Vernon held the creased parchment out to her.

She put up her hand as if to shield herself. "No, please. I don't want to touch it. Will you read it to me?"

Vernon studied her, his concern showing plainly on his face. "If this situation makes you uncomfortable, I can paraphrase what he says."

"No, no! I want to hear exactly what he wrote." She sat up straight against the cushions, gripping her hands together in her lap.

"Very well." Vernon cleared his throat and started to read.

Lady Emma,

Lord Dentley has insisted I write this missive to you in order to ease your concerns about the misunderstanding…

"That last is crossed out. He reluctantly changed the wording."

…the behavior I exhibited to you at the Seating's

ball. You and I have been close friends…

"I also requested a change to the last two words."

…acquaintances for a long time. I always admired you. I blame my conduct upon my sudden, intense attraction to you after being without your presence in my life for so many months.

"He insisted this is the true reason for his frenzied, hurtful treatment of you. He refused to alter the last sentence in any manner."

I hope you can forgive my demeanor when we last met, and we can remain friends…

"I insisted that he mark out those last few words."

I assure you that you need not be concerned about seeing me in the future.

Sir Charles Walling

Lady Emma sat still without speaking.

"It is obvious most of what he wrote did not come from the heart," her brother-in-law explained, with a sigh. "But I hope you can take comfort in the fact he does realize he overstepped the bounds of propriety with you at the ball. In his own distorted way, he is sorry for his actions."

"I believe our presence in London and our determination to confront him about the matter also made an impression on him," Lucas assured her. "He now understands we are serious when we tell him he needs to stay away from you and from Brighton."

Lady Emma slowly stood up from the settee. Lady Dentley rushed over to stand next to her. Vernon came to his feet as well.

She smiled with trembling lips as she put a hand to her forehead. "Thank you both for your efforts to relieve my mind of my worries about Sir Charles. Your comments and assurances on the matter are an immense help. This ordeal has exhausted me. I believe I will rest for a while in my room."

****

Emma got up early the following morning after a restless night. Although the news Vernon and Lord Millington brought her of Sir Charles had eased her concerns about the possibility of him trying to see her again, she couldn't help but deliberate again on the appalling events that had occurred at the ball. She tried to think of something else to distract her mind, but the effort proved fruitless. She finally rose from her bed, drawing her cotton wrapper around her body to ward off the morning chill before walking across the wooden floor on bare feet to the window.

The sun rose in a cloudless sky. Perhaps Celia would accompany her for a shopping expedition in town today. That should serve as a welcome diversion. She settled herself down in a chair by the window to attempt to read for a while.

"Good morning, Lady Emma." Her maid entered the room a short time later after a discreet knock on the door. "Here is your morning chocolate. What gown will you wear today?"

"Good morning. I am hoping to persuade my sister to join me in town." She mentally reviewed the dresses and pelisses she brought with her to Brighton. "I believe the Forester's green pelisse over the beige, cambric round garment and my matching green silk bonnet will serve nicely. In the meantime, help me put on the pink morning gown."

"Yes, my lady." Mary straightened the blankets and smoothed back the counterpane on the bed. Then she retrieved the morning gown, beige gown, and pelisse from the clothes' press and laid them on the coverlet.

She finished her chocolate and Mary assisted her with her morning toilet. Once her shift, stays, and petticoat were in place and her silk stockings on her legs, her maid lifted the morning gown over her head. For now, her maid brushed her hair into a simple bun. She slipped her feet into worn, gray kid slippers that were her favorite pair to wear around the house when she needn't be concerned about entertaining visitors.

"I will ring for you immediately after I finish my meal," she informed Mary, as she took one last look at her reflection in her mirror.

"Take your shawl, my lady. The dining room can be chilly in the mornings," warned her maid, handing over the favored, well-used garment.

They left the bedchamber together. Her maid headed toward the stairway leading to the servants' quarters. Emma walked around the corner to the main stairs and encountered Celia strolling down the hallway from her suite of rooms.

Emma stopped and forced a smile. "Good morning. I am going down to break my fast."

Celia came up to stand next to her, studying her intently. "Good morning, dear. How are you feeling this morning?"

"I am weary. I didn't sleep well. However, the prospect of staying indoors all day holds no appeal." Emma turned to lead the way. "I wish to visit the shops in town. Will you accompany me?"

"Oh, yes!" Celia answered happily. "There is a particular shade of ribbon I am searching for to replace the trim around the edge of the skirt on one of my favorite gowns."

"My lady, these are addressed to you." Worth bowed as they reached the main entry and handed her sister two envelopes, one quite noteworthy in its elegant, gold-embossed lettering.

"Thank you, Worth." Celia took the notes and then placed her free hand on Emma's arm. They walked together to the dining room.

"More invitations?" Emma inquired as their chairs were pulled back from the table by hovering footmen. "Who sent the uniquely decorated one?"

Celia sat down, picking up each of the envelopes, studying them. She suddenly dropped the one Emma indicated as if it were on fire. "My goodness! It is from the Prince Regent!"

"Whatever can it be? Were you expecting a royal summons?" She took a sip from the cup of tea a servant placed in front of her.

"No. Vernon hasn't said anything to me." Celia gingerly pulled the seal away from the envelope and took out the card wedged inside. "It's an invitation to a mid-morning breakfast at the Royal Pavilion the day after tomorrow!"

"How wonderful!" She spread some marmalade on a piece of toast. "I heard the interior is quite exotic. I am aware of the prince's penchant for unusual design and decoration. I can only imagine how unique it must be."

"You won't be required to wonder what it looks like." Celia took a sip of her tea. "The invitation includes your name."

Emma started in her seat when she heard the news. "How exciting! But you astound me; my name is actually on the invitation?"

"Yes, and our aunt's name as well; *Viscount and Viscountess Dentley, Mrs. Ruth Turner and Lady Emma Brenham.* It is common knowledge you both stay with us during the summer months. Oh, my! It should be a grand party!"

Emma frowned down at her plate. "I just recalled I never received any letters from Aunt Ruth. Did you hear from her?"

Celia carefully put the royal invitation back into the envelope. "No. I imagine she is busy visiting her many friends in Bath."

"You are probably correct." She picked up a piece of pound cake with her fork, from a dish in the center of the table and put it on her plate. "Hopefully, she is on her way here. It is a rare opportunity to be given the chance to attend one of the prince's parties."

"It is something she would certainly hate to miss," Celia agreed and took a bite of her toast before picking up the other envelope, breaking the seal on the back. She didn't speak for several moments while she perused the contents. "This is from an acquaintance of mine, a Lady Collins. I met her briefly in London. She is inviting you to a house party at the home of her son, Sir Edward."

"She is inviting me?" Emma dropped the remaining piece of cake on her plate and held out her hand. "Let me see that."

Lady Dentley,

You might remember our introduction by mutual friends while visiting the British Museum last year. I am organizing a small party of eligible ladies and gentlemen at my son Sir Edward's estate, Horsham House, in the hopes my daughter Camille will become better acquainted with a few gentlemen in a relaxed atmosphere before her formal come out next spring. In the spirit of 'the more the merrier' I thought of your unwed sister, Lady Emma Brenham. Please give her this invitation with my compliments. A welcome dinner is planned for a week from this Friday at Horsham House. I sincerely hope she will attend.

Lady Collins

Celia took a sip of her tea. "It sounds enjoyable."

"Enjoyable? It sounds like nothing more than a boring gathering of silly young people. The gentlemen will vie with each other to impress the most beautiful woman there. The ladies will simper and sigh over the most handsome man." Emma frowned down at the note. "There are obvious sticking points. I have never met Lady Collins. Will there be anyone attending I am acquainted with? How should I travel there?"

"You make it sound as if you are an old maid." Celia giggled. "The dinner is more than a week away. Perhaps you should wait a few days, to see if you hear a mutual acquaintance plans to go as well before you reply."

"I am not..." Emma stopped speaking, mentally scolding herself. She had intended to refuse to go without giving the outing any consideration at all. Turning down invitations had become too much of a habit. Should she wonder there were no offers for her from eligible gentlemen? Celia's assessment of the situation made sense. She should wait and make her decision in a couple of days.

"What were you going to say?" Her sister put the last bite of toast in her mouth.

"It is not important." Emma pushed back her chair and stood up. "This is an excellent reason to go shopping if we want to wear something special to the Prince

Regent's breakfast. I am going to change my gown."

Chapter Thirteen

"Should I instruct my driver to turn along the coast? It might be cooler there." Lucas gritted his teeth to keep from muttering an oath as well.

Lady Sophia Hampton twirled the frilly parasol she brought with her over her head. "I hesitate to agree to your suggestion, my lord. It is very sunny by the water. My complexion, you understand."

"Perhaps you would like to do some shopping?" He had offered to take Lady Sophia and Mrs. Wilcox for a drive to atone for the engagement he forgot several days before. He took advantage of the warm and sunny day. He borrowed his parents' barouche, telling James to put the top down. Upon observing Lady Sophia's less than enthusiastic relationship with the summer sunshine, he deeply regretted his choice of vehicle.

"Lord Millington, are Lady Dentley and Lady Emma coming out of the shop across the street?" Mrs. Wilcox indicated the spot with the tip of her cane.

He trained his gaze in the direction she indicated. Lady Emma looked particularly fine in a dark green pelisse. Additionally, an elaborate bonnet covered her hair with contrasting green silk rosettes ornamenting the crown. "Yes, it is! Lady Dentley! Lady Emma!"

The two women waved at him, walking toward the coach. He leaped down to greet them.

"So good to see you, Lord Millington," Lady

Dentley spoke out first. "Emma and I needed to purchase one or two items to augment our wardrobes."

Lady Emma followed behind her sister. "Hello, Mrs. Wilcox, Lady Sophia, and Lord Millington. Celia, I don't believe you were introduced. This is Lady Sophia Hampton, daughter of Lord and Lady Breech, my sister, Lady Dentley."

Lady Dentley inclined her head. "I am happy to make your acquaintance, Lady Sophia. Hello, Mrs. Wilcox."

"It is wonderful to see you both out and about." Mrs. Wilcox smiled warmly at the two ladies.

Lady Sophia gave her parasol a jaunty twirl, smiling down upon them with her full, red lips. "Lady Emma, I look forward to having the opportunity to speak to you quite often in the coming days."

"Indeed. What are you referring to?" she queried, with a frown.

"I extended my visit a few more weeks," Mrs. Wilcox spoke out. "I am told there is to be a house party at Sir Edward's home. Lady Breech and her daughter were invited. I understand you were petitioned to come as well, Lady Emma."

The two sisters exchanged meaningful looks before she said, "Who told you of my inclusion as a guest?"

"That person is me." Lucas cleared his throat. "Sir Edward is my good friend."

"I see. Well, I received the invitation just this morning. I am not certain if I will accept," Lady Emma replied in a straightforward, frank tone.

"I hope you will agree to come," said Mrs. Wilcox. "Unfortunately, Lady Breech fell and twisted her ankle yesterday. She will not be able to accompany her daughter. She asked I go to the event as her companion instead."

Lady Dentley gasped and turned to Lady Sophia. "I am terribly sorry to hear your mother is injured. I trust she is not in too much discomfort?"

"She is better today. Thank you for your concern. The swelling has gone down substantially. The doctor advised her to stay in bed for at least a week." Lady Sophia pursed her lips while fluttering her eye lashes managing, in Lucas' opinion, to appear indifferent to her mother's accident.

"A trial for anyone like her who leads an active life," he spoke up in a somber tone of voice, feeling genuinely sorry for the lady. "I am certain she will be counting the minutes until she can walk and ride again."

"It is indeed frustrating for my mother to lie about doing nothing." Lady Sophia gave a dramatic sigh. "Her horses are her life. Mrs. Wilcox and I visited the lending library this morning to collect several books for her perusal. She has her embroidery to keep her occupied as well."

"If you decide to accept the invitation, you are welcome to ride in my carriage," Lucas said to Lady Emma, wanting to change the subject as Lady Sophia's self-congratulatory attitude became intolerable. "I have extended my offer to the other two ladies. The lady's maids, my valet and groom will follow us with the baggage."

Lady Emma frowned, looking confused. "Are you certain there is room?"

"I plan to ride my horse to Horsham House," he informed her. "There is a good chance Edward and I will go riding and hunting during our visit."

"I think it is a wonderful notion." Lady Sophia trilled the words in her high-pitched, grating voice. "There...there isn't any chance of being robbed by highway men during our journey?"

"I am not aware of any danger on the road we are taking," he reassured her. "I will be riding just outside of the coach. Sir Edward's home is not far from here, about fifteen miles."

Lady Sophia let out a gusty sigh before replying in an equally dramatic manner, "You relieve my mind, my lord. I am concerned for your safety if such evil men should approach us without warning."

"I suggest we speak with Lord and Lady Breech first," interjected Mrs. Wilcox. "Your mother might have made plans to ride in someone else's equipage or perhaps they wish us to travel in their own carriage to the event."

Lady Sophia twirled her parasol and then pursed her lips into a pout before answering. "I cannot imagine any plans my mother might have made couldn't be changed. It would be much more amusing to ride in Lord Millington's carriage with Lady Emma."

"Amusing?" the lady in question challenged. "How does the image of riding in a carriage with me inspire mirth?"

Lady Sophia lowered the parasol, gazing intently at Lady Emma. "You misunderstand me. I believed it would be a diversion. Although you are older, I am certain you remain interested in the tremendously important matters that concern young ladies like me. We could compare notes on the latest fashions and opinions on eligible gentlemen."

Lucas became uneasy as he sensed an undercurrent of simmering anger in his companions. Lady Emma fumed. Lady Dentley watched the others with a look of tolerant amusement on her face. Mrs. Wilcox frowned. It was certainly time for him to turn on the charm and create a diversion. "It is such a nice, warm day. Would you ladies enjoy an ice? There is a new shop just off the Marine Parade called Rosetti's. I heard their lavender ice rivals Gunter's."

"It sounds simply divine; so smart of you to think of that." Lady Sophia flapped a gloved hand in his direction, giving him an expansive smile.

"I wanted to try their ice! Thank you!" exclaimed Lady Dentley, as she clapped her hands together.

"We need to inform our coachman of our change of plans." Lady Emma furrowed her brows. "Should we meet you there?"

"Where is he?" He stepped forward. "We can all go together. There is plenty of room in the coach. I will tell him where to meet us."

"Very well," Lady Emma sighed, pointing one gloved finger. "He is parked over there underneath the large elm tree."

"Let me help you both into the carriage first." He offered his hand to Lady Dentley, and then to Lady Emma. She gave him a speaking look as she settled herself on the seat next to Lady Sophia. He chose to ignore it, comprehending nothing could be explained in the presence of the others. "I will return in a moment."

After informing the Dentley coachman of their destination, Lucas hurried back to the carriage. Lady Sophia indicated a spot on the seat next to her by the door. "I saved you a place."

He wedged himself beside her as he called out instructions to the driver. The barouche moved through the bustling area that contained the shops, pubs and inns all frequented by summer visitors in Brighton.

"Oh, how adorable!" Lady Emma suddenly exclaimed.

"What is it?" asked her sister.

"See the sweet little girl with the mop of golden locks walking on the other side of the road with her nurse?" replied Lady Emma with a warm smile, keeping her gaze trained on the child. "She is dressed in her daytime finery; a primrose muslin gown, matching leather shoes, topped with a lovely coral necklace wrapped around her tiny neck."

"How very ingenuous! I had no notion you were interested in children's fashion," remarked Lady Sophia.

Lady Emma turned around to face her. "My enthusiasm is not only for the child's clothing. The little girl is precious. She reminds me of one of my dolls."

"You astound me!" Lady Sophia spoke the words in a superior manner. "If you find children so delightful, why haven't you married and started a brood of your own?"

Lady Emma blushed and turned away without making a reply.

Thankfully, the coachman brought the vehicle to a stop at that moment before tempers flared. They were parked across from a small building with a brightly colored sign over the door that read, *Delicious Ices, M. Rosetti, Proprietor*.

After waiting for the tiger to jump down and securely grip the horses' heads, he stood up, opened the carriage door and vaulted down into the street. "Does everyone want the lavender?"

A chorus of affirmatives answered his query. "Very

well; I will return shortly."

He strolled into the spotlessly clean shop, giving his order to the young girl behind the counter. Minutes later, he emerged carrying a tray with five dainty porcelain cups.

"Here you are, ladies." He walked up to the side of the coach, holding the ices out to them.

After they each secured their cups, Lucas picked up his own deciding to remain standing outside the carriage. No one spoke for several moments as they all spooned out the cold treat.

"Quite delicious!" exclaimed Mrs. Wilcox. "I never imagined a fragrance such as this could be made into an ice."

"Oh, no!" Lady Emma burst out as she frowned down at her chest. She had unbuttoned her pelisse earlier and a chunk of the ice had fallen to a spot just above her bodice. A trickle of moisture disappeared into the deep valley between her breasts. "How awkward this is."

"Oh, Emma!" Lady Dentley exclaimed as she stopped eating, moving forward in her seat. "What should we do?"

Lucas dropped his spoon into his cup, reaching into his waistcoat pocket for his handkerchief. He held it out. "Here, take this."

Lady Emma gave him a grateful, somewhat wobbly smile as she took the proffered square of material from his hand. She pressed the cloth against her exposed skin. Lucas promptly turned away. "At least it will dry quickly in this warm weather."

"It must be such a trial to you." Lady Sophia snickered inelegantly.

No one choose to reply to her crass innuendo. Lady

Emma reached out toward him with his handkerchief in her hand. "Thank you, my lord."

"I am glad to be of service." He forced himself to act nonchalant. He took a deep breath as he folded the piece of cloth, stuffing it back into his pocket.

Mrs. Wilcox cleared her throat before speaking. "What other flavors are favorites?"

"I consider pineapple to be second best." He swallowed the last spoonful of ice into his mouth. He fervently hoped the treat cooled down the lustful reactions he was experiencing in another part of his body.

"I have never sampled any flavor but this one." Lady Sophia daintily patted her lips with her own lace-trimmed handkerchief. "I am told it has soothing qualities to one's middle region."

Mrs. Wilcox frowned, looking confused. "Middle region?"

Lady Emma chuckled. "I believe Lady Sophia is alluding to the stomach. British ladies are taught to avoid mentioning specific body parts in polite conversation."

"Emma!" Lady Dentley gasped.

"No matter. I hardly think she has lowered herself to commoner status simply by clarifying a word choice for her American friend," Lucas assured her. He gathered the spoons and empty cups, returning them to an outside table set up especially for their collection.

"I believe we should go back and check on Lady Breech," advised Mrs. Wilcox.

"I need to return home before my sons wake from their naps." Lady Dentley clutched her reticule tightly on her lap. "I make a point to check on them in the afternoons."

"I trust your lads are doing well?" Lucas inquired, as he approached the carriage.

Lady Dentley smiled at him before replying. "They are fine, thank you. When my sons are with their governess, I never need to worry."

"The woman is a paragon," Lucas quipped.

"I would be lost without her," agreed Lady Dentley.

Lady Emma stood up. "I see our coach is parked close by."

"Let me escort you both to your carriage." He opened the door, helping them step to the ground.

Mrs. Wilcox and Lady Sophia called their goodbyes. He offered both ladies an arm. They crossed the street, coming abreast of the Dentley vehicle. Their groom held open the door. Lady Dentley entered first.

"Did you make plans for other outings in the coming days?" he asked Lady Emma, reluctant to see her leave.

She moved forward to step inside the coach then stopped on the threshold, turning around. "Yes, my sister informed me this morning we were invited to a mid-morning breakfast as the Regent's guests at the Royal Pavilion the day after tomorrow."

"Excellent!" He grinned at her. "My parents and I received an invitation as well. Have you ever visited the Pavilion?"

"No, I have never been there. I understand the prince recently started some extensive construction." She looked at him with shining eyes. "I am excited to see the improvements."

He became conscious of a sense of great satisfaction. Her comments demonstrated her understanding of events and happenings outside of her own personal life. He shared her enthusiasm and thirst

137

for knowledge. "I attended an event last summer at the invitation of the Regent. He wished to show off the new kitchen to us. The room is one of the first designed and completed by John Nash."

"The kitchen? It is hard to believe you are interested in that particular room," she told him in a skeptical tone.

He raised his eyebrows, staring fixedly at her when he heard her somewhat cynical inflection. "As a matter of fact, I observed many unique features. Nash did much to make certain the heavy demands for elaborate meals the prince makes upon his array of French chefs, whenever he is in residence in Brighton, were met in the most efficient, effective manner."

Her eyes widened. She looked dubious. "Indeed? Could you describe how such a thing is accomplished?"

"The kitchen is located within a convenient distance to the banqueting room, for one. No more hot dishes arrive at the table cold because of long, draughty corridors. The room itself is light and airy with high ceilings and many windows," he informed her. "There is also a constant supply of water to the kitchen from a tower on the property. Additionally, there are separate cooking stations with plenty of counter space to assemble the extravagant dishes Prinny's present chef is reputed for."

She frowned at him, lifting her chin. "You sound as if you speak from experience when you make note of the importance of the kitchen being in close proximity to the dining room. Are you much involved with these issues in your own household?"

"Yes, I am," he acknowledged with pride. "I make a point to do everything I can to ensure every aspect on my small estate is run as efficiently as possible. Thankfully,

I employ a competent staff. They make certain this happens on a daily basis whether I am in residence or not."

"You surprise me." She cocked her head, studying him intently. The green silk rosettes on her bonnet glistened in the sunlight. "I pictured you as an absentee landlord; trusting your secretary or steward to make most of the decisions directly affecting your estate."

A stiff breeze blew off the ocean. The sudden gust carried the aroma of Lady Emma's sweet, lemony scent to him. He gave her a lopsided, teasing grin. The exchange reminded him of the previous enjoyable repartee at their initial chance meeting in London. "Surely you don't believe my life is devoted solely to seeking pleasure?"

She met his gaze, answering him in a serious tone. "You cannot blame me for having that impression. I understand you value your independence, and you carry an aversion to marriage. To me, those two qualities make one think of a confirmed bachelor who spends his days occupied with frivolous pursuits. Why would I ever believe running an estate a priority with a person such as I described?"

"This conversation is quite diverting, Emma, but we need to head for home." Lady Dentley poked her head out of the coach window.

"Oh! I am so sorry, Celia!" Her face flushed as she offered her gloved hand to him. "Good-bye, my lord."

"My apologies, Lady Dentley." He gripped her elbow, helping her into the carriage. "Please accept the invitation to the house party, Lady Emma. I'll make a bargain with you. If you attend, I will do my best to see we finish our conversations."

Chapter Fourteen

The groom lowered the steps at the carriage door. He stood close by to offer help if needed to her and her sister. Vernon exited behind them and took his wife's hand, pausing to confer with his coachman where best to park their vehicle.

After she navigated the steps with the groom's assistance, Emma stood to the side of the driveway, waiting for her companions. She smoothed down the front of her garment with her hand, one of her favorites, a long-sleeved, soft peach-colored walking gown. She wore it with a matching spencer ornamented with thick braiding at the edges. A leghorn hat she had purchased the day before covered her head. The brim turned up to frame her face, the crown was decorated with four rows of peach-colored satin and trimmed in white cord.

"We are ready," announced Vernon, as he and Celia walked up to her side.

She studied the swarm of people gathered near the main entrance to the Pavilion. "Shall we stroll along the front walkway for a time to allow the receiving line to diminish in size?"

"Lady Emma!"

She turned around at the sound of a familiar voice. "Lord Millington! I wondered if you were already inside."

He openly studied her. "You look charming."

To her great embarrassment, she blushed. "Th... Thank you, my lord."

He turned to greet Vernon and Celia. "Please meet my parents, Earl and Countess Watford. Father, Mother, this is Lord and Lady Dentley. Lady Dentley is Lady Emma's sister."

The countess acknowledged the introductions with a haughty nod of her head. "Lord Dentley. I previously made the acquaintance of your wife."

To break up the awkward silence that followed this condescending remark, Emma commented, "We were discussing a quandary; should we stroll in the gardens for a time and wait for the crowds to lessen?"

"We might as well join the masses at the door." The countess sighed and reached a gloved hand up to adjust a feather plume on her hat. "I cannot imagine the prince will dawdle overly long with his greetings. Don't you agree, Thomas?"

Lord Watford mov ed next to his wife, placing her hand on his arm. "The sooner we get through the line, the quicker we will be served. I admit to feeling a bit peevish. The small plate of eggs and kippers didn't fill me up this morning."

"You were wise not to overindulge, Father. You are well aware of the abundant, sumptuous meals the prince instructs his famous chefs to serve at events such as these," Lord Millington pointed out.

Celia and Vernon moved to the front of their group, Lord and Lady Watford followed them. Lord Millington joined Emma to bring up the rear.

"Such a pity Lady Sophia couldn't join us." Lady Watford twisted around to look at Emma. "You knew her mother fell down a few days ago? Dutiful daughter that

141

she is, Lady Sophia chose to forego the party today to stay at home to assist Lord Breech in keeping her spirits up."

"Very admirable, I am sure," replied Emma.

Lady Watford yanked on her husband's arm, forcing him to come to a stop. "Are you being sarcastic? Do you believe she should be here?"

"Mother! Please!" Lord Millington glared at her.

"I never imagined mocking Lady Sophia's decision to keep her mother company. I would do the same thing myself," she told the countess, not mincing her words.

"My dear, this discussion is better saved for another time." Lord Watford gripped his wife's hand, urging her along. "We are holding up the line."

Lord Millington put his hand on Emma's arm, halting her as his parents moved forward. "I apologize for my mother. Those comments are uncalled for."

She took a deep breath. "Lady Watford is upset. Is there something wrong?"

A gentleman standing behind them cleared his throat and they advanced once more, keeping the line of eager guests behind them moving. Lord Millington murmured to her, "Please disregard what she said. You previously experienced her gruff mannerisms. Outspoken is a generous description of her personality. She is taking her frustrations out on you. I believe she hoped Lady Sophia and I would further our acquaintance today."

"I see," Emma answered, intently studying his face, noting his reserved demeanor. "I must be a poor substitute in her eyes."

"Not ever in mine." Lord Millington murmured. He reached out to stroke her cheek with one gloved finger. He suddenly smiled at her, his intense blue orbs glowing like jewels. "Come. You have never been to the Pavilion. Allow me to point out a few items of interest to you."

She savored the warm, tingly sensations coursing throughout her body when Lord Millington caressed her and so earnestly inferred he experienced happiness in her company. She tamped down the heady response, vowing to cherish it later in the privacy of her bedchamber. She made herself to concentrate on the building before her. "T…Thank you. I hope not to miss anything of importance."

"We were here for a tour shortly after Nash began remodeling the Pavilion in 1816," Celia remarked as she and Vernon strolled up to them.

It happened Emma was fortunate enough to be the first person in their group to walk through the doors into the entrance hall. She stopped short only a few paces inside with her head tilted back and her mouth open.

"Quite detailed, is it not?" Lord Millington remarked at her side.

"Oh, yes!" She studied the painted dragons adorning the walls above the front windows and the globular lamps that hung at the corners of the ceilings. The soft green walls with their intricate cornices at the ceiling and the plush carpet covering the floor added an alluring touch to the strikingly glamourous room. "I heard the prince never misses any important aspects when he decorates the interiors of his homes, but this is astonishing. It is like an exotic fairy tale come to life."

Lord Millington chuckled. "I couldn't describe the experience any better."

"And to think the Pavilion is still far from being finished," commented Vernon.

"I do hope we are invited back to see it when it is

completed," said Celia, in a wistful tone.

"It could be several years, my dear," Vernon pointed out. "The Prince is forever coming up with new ideas for its ornamentation."

"I am willing to wait," declared Celia. "His parties are legendary. I'm certain this breakfast will be something to remember."

"I can't imagine improving on what is already here," observed Emma.

"This is only a taste of the elaborate details on display in the subsequent rooms," clarified Lord Millington. "Did you notice the sabre-leg chairs with the scroll-framed backs?"

"In green leather, no less," added Vernon.

A regally uniformed footman walked up to their group and bowed. "My lords and ladies, I will take your coats and hats. The prince awaits you in the Blue Drawing Room."

They handed over the various articles of clothing before making their way out of the hall into the next room.

Lord Millington offered his arm to Emma. She placed her hand on his sleeve as he guided her forward. "This area is called The Corridor or the Long Gallery, a type of interior promenade. You will notice the hexagonal lanterns with painted glass panels and silk tassels. These illuminate the corridor at night while the tinted skylights overhead allow muted light to come in during the daytime."

"It's beautiful. The plants on the walls; they are very thin and graceful. They look like a type of reed." She stopped to study one elaborate cluster.

"Those plants are meant to depict bamboo." Lord

Millington indicated a group of chairs propped against the wall. "These are made of Chinese bamboo."

She reached out to carefully touch the curved arm on one of the chairs. "I would think such a thin reed would not be strong enough to be made into furniture, but it appears to be very sturdy material."

"I believe there are many different types of bamboo; some are more durable than others." He smiled down at her. "What do you think of the murals?"

"So lovely; the dusky, pink walls, the light blue images of waving bamboo and flying birds." She sighed. "At night; with the lanterns lit, it must be exquisite."

"Your sister looks as if she greatly admires the interior as well," Lord Millington observed.

"I told Vernon it reminds me of an indoor Vauxhall Garden with an Oriental flair, don't you agree, Emma?"

"Yes, there is a similarity, but Vauxhall could never compete with all these lavish, exotic details."

"Only the prince could pull something of this magnitude off," Vernon remarked.

"And find a way to pay for it," Lord Millington added, with a grimace.

Another footman waited for them at an open doorway to one side of the corridor. He bowed deeply before rising and asking for their names. He turned away, speaking loudly into the room. "Your Royal Highness, may I present to you, Viscount and Viscountess Dentley, Viscount Millington and Lady Emma Brenham."

"Welcome, please come inside." The footman bowed once more and moved aside for them to enter.

Emma peered around Vernon's shoulder to see the Regent, wearing his red coat decorated with the Royal Seal on the left side and the Royal blue sash draped across an intricate silver and black waistcoat. His stomach protruded out from beneath this article of clothing, the buttons straining against their fastenings. He lounged back against an overstuffed armchair placed in the center of the room. A crystal goblet half full of a golden-hued liquid, presumably brandy, rested on an ornate table at his side. In one of his hands, he clasped a white piece of linen. He used the scrap of material to languidly wipe at the sweat beading upon his forehead. Emma recalled hearing the prince held a fear of drafty rooms. A large fire roared and crackled in the grate not far from his chair.

Lord Millington spoke softly into her ear. "You and your family greet him first. I will follow."

"Lady Emma, welcome." The prince spoke with a booming voice, the sound reverberated throughout the room. "And Lord and Lady Dentley as well. I believe Lady Dentley is your sister, my dear?"

Emma curtsied in front of the prince. He reached out as Emma came to her feet. She placed her gloved hand in his before answering. Thankfully, her voice came out steady and clear. "Yes, Your Royal Highness, she is."

"I am told this is the first time you visited the Pavilion. What do you think of it?"

She didn't speak for a moment as she studied an intricate cabinet where fine porcelain and mandarin figures were on display against the wall directly behind the prince. "The word that comes to mind is enchanting, Sire. The hanging lanterns, the elegant bamboo furniture, the columns, and patterned pilasters framing the recesses and detailed canopies set above the windows, the wallpaper covered with flowering trees and birds. It is a feast for the eyes."

The prince gasped for breath as he chortled out loud. "A feast for the eyes, you say! Brilliant! You have made me incredibly happy, Lady Emma. Please enjoy my home while you are visiting."

"I'm honored to be here as your guest, Your Royal Highness." She curtsied close to the ground once more before being guided away by a hovering footman.

Chapter Fifteen

That certainly went well, thought Lucas as he watched the prince greet the others from his spot near the doorway to the Blue Room.

"Lord and Lady Dentley, welcome." The prince dropped his handkerchief to his lap and picked up the goblet of brandy. He took a noisy gulp of the liquid before continuing, "How are your two sons? Off to Cambridge yet?"

"No, Sire," Lord Dentley cleared his throat. "They are a little young for college."

"We employ a fine governess who tutors them at present, Sire," added Lady Dentley.

"Well, all in good time. Enjoy them now while they are boisterous, eager lads." The prince nodded, and a footman led them away. He turned to look directly at Lucas. "Lord Millington, Watford and his countess informed me you were in attendance."

He walked forward, bowing low. "Your Royal Highness. I would never miss an event held here at the Pavilion."

"I am glad to hear you say so." The prince put his goblet down on the table and gestured to him. "Come closer."

He moved to his side. "Yes, Sire?"

The prince cupped his pudgy hand around his chin and whispered, "Aren't you Venetia's protector?"

Startled by the query, he couldn't think what to reply. After several unlikely possibilities flitted through his mind, he settled for the truth. "Uh, no more, Sire. I gave her up when I came to Brighton."

"Oh. What a great shame! Such a beautiful lady with an exceedingly lovely voice." The prince leaned a little closer. "No doubt very expensive as well."

"I…I am certain you are aware, Sire, the more in favor they are, the greater the cost," he answered, thinking it was a very strange conversation to be having with the prince.

"Naturally!" The prince smiled smugly with his protruding lips before waving him away.

Lucas bowed once more before heading to the next room as another group of people were announced.

****

A few minutes later, when everyone sat at the large banquet table, the prince sauntered into the room. Conversations and laughter ringing out across the room immediately stopped.

"Welcome everyone! Please enjoy the scrumptious food my talented chef and his staff prepared. If there is a chance after you finish your meal, take a visit to the kitchen. I am quite proud of what has been accomplished there. It is something of a marvel. There are heat-powered roasting spits, huge, cast-iron stewing stoves, hot cupboards to keep food warm, steam dressers and tables that are fed by concealed pipes running underneath them. There are sinks with hot and cold running water as well. Everything required to roast or boil, bake stew, fry, steam, or heat is provided in a well-aired, high-ceilinged room that is near the dining room. You will never need to suffer the indignity of sipping lukewarm soup or eating cold vegetables when you dine here. We hope the new Banqueting Room is complete and open in a few months."

Loud applause sounded across the entire room.

"I also wish to inform you the Great Dome is going to be installed in a fortnight. It will be centered over the Saloon and eventually connect the Music and Banqueting rooms. We constructed an iron cage to support the iron framework on the dome. Come and join me as I observe the installation. It should be quite an exciting event. Now, enjoy your breakfast and be sure to tour the house and grounds when you are finished. As most of you comprehend, I rarely rise from my bed before three in the afternoon. I must resume my rest. I bid you farewell until we meet again."

With that speech, the prince turned and left the room to the sound of more thunderous applause. Moments later, a swarm of footmen entered from a side doorway, carrying large trays of food resting on the palms of their upturned hands and other dishes hovering precariously above their heads. More waiters followed carrying bottles of champagne.

Emma marveled at the speed at which the servants served all the guests. She studied her full plate as she dropped her serviette in her lap and reached for her fork. Other than the usual breakfast fare of eggs, bacon, and toast, there were more unique dishes of pigeon and ham pie, slices of roasted lamb, and pieces of grilled fillet of sole, all accompanied by carrots, onions, and potatoes. And just as the prince promised, a rising steam coming off the food in front of her proved all the dishes were as piping hot now as they were when they left the stove or oven.

"I hope you are hungry." The sound of Lord Millington's voice at her side halted her contemplation of the food.

She turned to find him grinning down at her. She smiled in return. "I will certainly do my best to do justice to this enormous meal. I notice how well-trained the prince's servants are. They served over fifty people a vast amount of food in a short amount of time."

"It helps if you employ an army of footmen continually at your beck and call," he countered.

"It is a novel idea to locate the kitchen so close to the dining room," Celia commented, seated on Emma's other side, "I imagine the odors permeate to other rooms?"

"You forget, my dear, the prince said the kitchen has a high ceiling and is well-aired," Vernon reminded his wife from his position next to her. "I imagine the smells from the cooking are pushed to the outside fairly quickly and never reach the other areas of the Pavilion."

"He proved correct when he promised our breakfast would be served hot." Emma bit into a piece of fish, chewing slowly to savor the flavor.

"I am interested to see exactly how the process works, the steam tables and hot cupboards that the prince spoke of. The pipes were not installed when I received my initial tour of the kitchen," Lord Millington observed before turning back to his plate.

Vernon paused in the act of spreading some jam on a piece of bread. "I noticed the prince displayed a fervent intention to speak to you in the Blue Room. Was it important?"

Lord Millington didn't immediately answer. He cleared his throat and hesitated before replying.

"He...He wanted to question me."

"Did he inquire about your estate?" Vernon took a bite of his bread.

Lord Millington made a noise in his throat and took a sip of his champagne. "No. He asked after someone I used to be acquainted with."

"Someone well thought of?" Vernon picked up a piece of bacon.

Lord Millington looked away, appearing to study the other occupants at the crowded table before turning back. "The person is not generally discussed. The answer is best left unsaid at this time."

Lady Watford spoke up from across the table. "The prince made a point to inquire if you were in attendance when he greeted us. But he made no mention of having anything of import to ask you."

At her side, Lord Watford took a generous bite of his meat pie, chewed, and swallowed before commenting, "Precisely because the subject is personal in nature, my dear, and not for our ears."

"As I informed Lord Dentley, Mother, it is a private matter," Lord Millington retaliated. He discouraged further questions when he bent over his plate and speared some egg with his fork.

"Very well, I won't belabor the issue. Lady Emma, tell me about your kitchen in your home in London. Is it quite small?" Lady Watford glared at her with her knife and fork suspended over her plate, as if daring her to say otherwise.

Emma swallowed a piece of potato. "No, my kitchen is fairly large. There is ample space for the fireplace, as well as a small brick range, a cast iron oven, sink, and a hot closet. We placed a broad worktable in the center of the room."

Lady Watford raised her eyebrows. "Indeed. I am surprised. You are fortunate. I imagine you are the hostess of frequent dinner parties?"

"No, very infrequently," Emma countered. "My Aunt Ruth and I entertain on occasion, but generally we read or embroider in the evenings."

"Your Aunt Ruth..., is she your mother's sister?" Lady Watford reached for her goblet but didn't drink from it.

"Mrs. Ruth Turner. No. She is my father's sister," she countered. The woman needed a target in her quest for exclusive information, and it was obvious she had been chosen as the bull's eye. Emma's appetite disappeared. She placed her utensils in the center of her plate pushing it away before wiping her mouth with the serviette.

"She did not accompany you on your visit to your sister's home here?" Lady Watford raised her glass to her lips.

"My aunt is staying with friends in Bath, where she lived before becoming widowed." Emma stiffened her spine and sat ramrod straight against the back of her chair. "I am certain you will wish to inquire as to her deceased husband's background. Mr. Turner owned a reputable jewelry store in that city."

Lady Watford sputtered as she choked on her champagne. She waved away her husband's offer of assistance, lowering her goblet to the table. "You are an impertinent woman!"

"I see no harm in anticipating your question," Emma clarified as she reached for her glass. After sipping the rest of the liquid, she placed the goblet down, dropped her serviette to the table, and came to her feet. "I cannot eat another morsel. Would you like to take a stroll in the gardens with me, Celia?"

"Excuse me? Uh no, no thank you," her sister responded with surprise, "I asked Vernon to accompany me to the kitchens."

"I will be happy to escort you outside." Lord Millington stood up and offered her his arm.

She frowned at him. "I believed you intended to look at the steam tables."

"We can study those after we finish our walk outside." He smiled at her. "But only if that is agreeable to you, of course."

"Very well. I need to locate someone to retrieve my spencer and hat first." She turned and headed toward the double doors leading to the garden. A footman standing at attention nearby sprinted over to swing them open. She stepped out, took a deep breath of warm, salty air, and then studied the arrangement of plants as they spread out before her, attempting to calm her anger at Lady Watford's callous treatment.

Lord Millington hovered behind her. He gently squeezed her arm. "Wait here. I will ask a servant to bring your garments."

"Thank you." She contemplated the scenery as she waited for him to return. In front of her, a wide pathway ringed the rim of a large, grassy area. To the right, she could make out clusters of daisies and buttercups.

Moments later, Lord Millington joined her. He held her spencer for her while she placed the hat onto her head, tying the ribbon underneath her chin. As he helped her maneuver her arms into the sleeves of the spencer, she caught a whiff of his favored cologne, the poignant and spicy aroma of sandalwood. She turned to face him, relishing the fragrance. "I appreciate your assistance. Thank you."

He bowed his head to her and smiled. "You are very welcome. Where shall we go first?"

She pointed toward the flowers. "Let us make our way over there."

He murmured his agreement and they strolled along the path. "I must apologize for my mother once again."

She studied him before replying, "There is no need. I know how to deal with her excessive forthrightness."

He chuckled. "That is an excellent way to describe her unfortunate disposition. How do you propose to handle her?"

"I will simply outdo her by being more caustic than she is," she explained. "When I sense she is about to strike out with one of her scathing comments, I will take the sting out of her observation by making an outrageous statement of my own."

He slowed his stride, appearing to ponder her words. "Hmm…it just might work."

"I believe she will think twice before making any cutting remarks to me," she confided. When they reached a group of bright yellow daisies, she stopped to bend over one of the flowers. She rubbed her chin against a few of the petals. "They are so soft."

"But never as soft as your silken cheeks." He murmured the words into her ear.

She pulled away from him with a sigh. "Oh, how easily the honeyed words trip off your tongue!"

He frowned down at her. "What is that supposed to mean?"

Drat her waywardness! She should remember never

to speak her thoughts out loud. She hesitated to answer his query. She had to explain herself and it promised to be awkward. "The other day…when we were talking with Mrs. Wilcox and Lady Sophia, I watched you work your magic with the silly, feather-brained girl; why, you practically made her eat out of your hand with a few well-mannered remarks and some glowing smiles! So much so that by the time we parted from them, Lady Sophia couldn't imagine traveling to the house party with anyone but you as her escort. I warn you, I'm not so impressionable, my lord. Your reputation proceeds you. I comprehend you are a practiced flirt."

He crossed his arms in front of his broad chest and scowled at her. "I am surprised by your comments. I never thought my actions appeared so. I can promise you, when I spoke to Lady Sophia, I had nothing more in mind than your need of female companionship on the journey to Edward's estate. I hoped the two of you would form a friendship, providing you the comfort of an acquaintance once we arrived at the party."

She couldn't help the unladylike grunt that came out of her mouth before she replied, "Your answer shows how little you understand me. I am not claiming to be the most brilliant woman in England, but surely you cannot imagine I would find it easy to converse with such an empty-headed, self-centered girl for three hours inside the tight quarters of a carriage!"

He reached out to grasp her forearm. "I am sorry. I am aware you consider Mrs. Wilcox a good friend; she would also keep you company. I admit I believed you would enjoy discussing the latest fashions with Lady Sophia during the journey."

She glared at him. "You forgot, she also proposed to

speak of my *opinions on eligible gentlemen.*"

He chuckled. "That comment slipped my mind. Well, play along with her and compare notes."

She tapped her foot on the ground in frustration. "I don't have any notes to compare!"

He raised his eyebrows. "What? Surely there are numerous gentlemen who captured your notice in London."

"No. The only notices I receive are the lewd, whispered comments by those men who make fun of my…my shape," she murmured her answer while staring at the ground, willing herself not to cry.

His gloved hand moved into her line of vision. He put his fingers underneath her chin, gently guiding her face upward until she looked directly at him. "I apologize for those boorish louts who call themselves gentlemen. Unfortunately, in our society, any unmarried lady is understood to be without protection. She becomes fair game to the drunken simpletons who find a kind of sick humor and twisted self-importance in making single women embarrassed and discomfited."

She stayed quiet, savoring his touch, while she pondered his reply. "I'm sorry, but it strikes me as very wrong when you explain the situation in that way."

He lowered his hand, frowning. "No one ever said societies' dictates made sense. Is your brother-in-law aware of what is said to you?"

"Vernon? No. I…I never told him. I…I feared he would feel constrained to defend my honor and challenge someone to a duel," she clarified. "I would never put him in such a quandary. I must think of my sister and nephews. The risk of loss of life is too great to fight over drunken remarks that most forget they uttered by morning."

He reached for her hand, squeezing it gently. "Don't pay any attention to those idiots. They made you doubt yourself. Remember you are intelligent, sweet, and lovely. Concentrate on those wonderful traits and not the other hurtful things that were said."

She gripped his hand in her own, relishing his words as well as his strength, smiling up at him. "Thank you for saying such nice things about me, my lord. I might forgive you for consigning me to a three-hour carriage ride with Lady Sophia."

He grinned. "Hopefully, the experience won't turn out to be as bad as you think."

She made a face at him. "It will probably be worse."

Chapter Sixteen

"Lord Millington! Would you like to join us inside? There is plenty of room."

Lucas looked up from his contemplation of the roadside vegetation to see Lady Sophia hanging out of one of the carriage windows, waving her white embroidered handkerchief at him. He nudged his horse's flanks with his thighs to steer the animal closer to the vehicle. "No, thank you. There is only a short distance to go. Did you complete your discussion of this year's fashions so soon?"

Lady Sophia rolled her eyes and sighed before responding, "Lady Emma doesn't bother herself overly much with such things. After agreeing with me on where to buy the finest satin and giving her opinion on the best dressmaker in London, she has been plying Mrs. Wilcox with queries about the United States. I believe the advantages of living on the coast in a busy port city are now being compared to the peace and quiet of the countryside."

"Traveling to other countries holds no interest for you?"

The lady pondered his question. "The image of being cooped up inside of a tiny cabin on a ship that is frequently tossed about in a haphazard manner in a churned-up ocean, holds no glamour for someone with such tender sensibilities as I carry, my lord."

"Perhaps a trip to Paris by way of a well-sprung traveling carriage would be more pleasurable?"

"I admit, visiting a sophisticated city like Paris does appeal to me. The wardrobe I could obtain there would quickly overshadow the ladies here who consider themselves the arbiters of the latest styles." She waved her handkerchief in a dramatic fashion across her cheek before clutching it in the palm of her hand. "But, alas, I fear I must admit to you I am a creature who greatly values life's comforts. With such a placid constitution as I possess, I cannot tolerate days upon days of movement whether inside an elegant carriage or on a ship floating upon the calmest of waters."

"I am sorry to hear that. Motion sickness can indeed make any journey a miserable experience." He stared intently at the opposite coach window, in hopes Lady Emma would poke her head out and save him from prolonged conversation with the vapid Lady Sophia.

"Did I give you the impression I suffered from such a malady? I assure you I am made up of the strongest of constitutions!" She tugged on the crumpled handkerchief until it fluttered daintily once more from her fingertips. "I simply meant to imply I need to be grounded. I follow a daily routine that brings me comfort and serenity. It is extremely arduous to pamper myself while traveling."

Apparently, Lady Sophia contained a confusing mixture of tender sensibilities combined with a strong constitution. He debated how to discuss such extreme opposites in character when the lady herself suddenly changed the subject.

"Are you aware who else is invited to the party, my lord?" A few wrinkles showed on her smooth forehead. "I find myself in a quandary. I brought four trunks of gowns. If I should require additional garments, it would prove to be extremely awkward to obtain them. We are so far from any dressmakers of quality or of good reputation."

He experienced a startling image of Lady Sophia pleading with him to be her escort back to town to collect more clothing. He hastened to reassure her. "I understand from Sir Edward, this event started as his mother's idea. She wished for Camille to meet a few eligible gentlemen in a relaxed setting before she begins her season in London. You shouldn't need to replenish your wardrobe."

The opposite window on the carriage opened at that moment. He breathed a hearty sigh of relief when he saw Lady Emma's bonneted head emerge from within.

"Are we far from Horsham House, my lord? Mrs. Wilcox needs to stretch her legs. Her knee is getting stiff."

He studied the wide lane bordered by elm trees up ahead. "I believe there is less than a mile to go. Shall I tell the driver to stop?"

"Let me ask her." She disappeared back inside the carriage only to reappear moments later. "She assures me she is perfectly able to withstand such a short distance."

"We can pull over anytime if need be." He resisted losing her contribution to the discussion. He posed a question to her, "Tell me, Lady Emma, how many trunks of clothes did you happen to bring on this adventure?"

She regarded him with confusion before answering, "I brought two. Is there a reason you need to comprehend such a thing, my lord?"

He cleared his throat before replying. "Lady Sophia is concerned she hasn't brought enough gowns with her.

Since she has four trunks of garments, I can now reassure her she will have more than enough during our stay."

"Not necessarily." Lady Sophia's hand gripped the window ledge as the carriage bounced over a rut in the road. "Proper garments that adapt to my mood as well as the occasion are particularly important to me. Since I believed the event to be a casual gathering with immediate neighbors, I brought mostly brightly colored, unadorned gowns, apart from a beaded puce colored one in case there is dancing. Camille never mentioned several eligible gentlemen would be attending. How am I to impress in such plain garments?"

He directed his gaze to Lady Emma with a clear message of desperation in his expression and a silent plea for her assistance. It appeared she read his unspoken appeal when she promptly replied, "I am sure your gowns will be most suitable. Certainly, the gentlemen will barely notice what you are wearing when they are confronted by your resplendent beauty."

"You are correct." Lady Sophia thrust out her chin, pulling the brim of her bonnet back off her face as if inviting them to stare at her features. "How can a simple garment compare to a visage such as mine?"

"Indeed." Lady Emma turned to frown at him before backing inside the carriage once more.

At that moment, the vehicle moved to the right as it entered the avenue leading to Horsham House. Lucas sat up straighter in the saddle, sighing with great contentment. They had arrived at their destination. He could now avoid being the direct recipient of any more of Lady Sophia's absurd comments and ridiculous queries. Hard-pressed to keep the resonance of giddiness out of his voice, he announced, "We are here at last, ladies!"

****

Emma covertly studied Lady Sophia as she glided down the steps of the carriage, helped to the ground by a footman. She turned back to call out, "I will inform our hostess we arrived."

Emma stood up, offering her hand to Mrs. Wilcox. The lady took it with a grateful smile, slowly rising to her feet. "I am so sorry you were made to endure that silly female's chatter throughout the entire excursion."

"I admit I wondered how I would tolerate her company inside a carriage for an extended period of time." She chuckled. "You observed, once I refused to participate further on the subject of gowns and fashion and turned to you to hear more about your life in the United States, she quickly became bored. I am grateful Lord Millington kept her preoccupied during the final leg of our journey."

Mrs. Wilcox made her way to the carriage door. "I glanced at her periodically, intending to engage her in conversation. Either she lay back against the squabs with her eyes closed or stared out of the window. It is often hard for me to think of something of interest to discuss with her."

Emma waited to reply until the footman assisted both herself and Mrs. Wilcox to retrieve various items left on the seats deemed necessary to take with them on the trip. Once that was accomplished, they shook out their creased skirts and walked toward the front of the house. "In the brief period of time since I met Lady Sophia, I have determined there are a limited number of topics she enjoys speaking about."

"Ladies, allow me to introduce you to our host, Sir

Edward Collins. Edward, this is Lady Emma Brenham and Mrs. Wilcox. Mrs. Wilcox is visiting from the United States."

Emma turned at the sound of Lord Millington's voice to find him standing directly behind them. At his side stood a tall, handsome gentleman with a crop of tousled curly black hair and very green eyes.

"A pleasure, Sir Edward." Emma curtsied to him. "I understand you and Lord Millington are good friends."

"That is correct. We have known each other for quite a while." Sir Edward bowed over her hand. "It is wonderful you could join us. My mother has implied this party is mainly for the benefit of my sister, Camille. Several eligible gentlemen as well as Camille's particular lady friends from her finishing school were invited. We three must stick together and make up our own party."

He turned to Mrs. Wilcox. "I hope you are enjoying your trip in our country."

"Yes, indeed I am. I'm sorry, bad knee, very awkward, can't curtsey." She clasped her cane in her left hand, thrusting out her right one. "I am glad to make your acquaintance. I am here as companion to Lady Sophia Hampton as a favor to her mother. Lord and Lady Breech are friends of mine. I have been staying with them. Lady Breech fell and twisted her ankle a few days ago. I hope you don't mind I came in her stead."

"No problem at all." Sir Edward shook her outstretched hand. "My mother will be busy entertaining all of us. She will appreciate any assistance keeping the young people on their best behavior as well. I trust Lady Breech is recovering?"

"Yes, she is. When we left, the swelling had gone

down and most of the pain had subsided. I will write and tell her you asked after her." She shifted her cane back and forth on the ground, wincing. "I am sorry. I'm quite stiff from sitting in the carriage for so long a time."

Sir Edward kept his hold on Mrs. Wilcox's hand and placed it on his sleeve. "Get a good grip on my arm, ma'am. I overheard Lady Sophia asking my housekeeper to show her to her room so she could *repair the damages from the journey*. Would you like to go to your bedchamber as well, or do you feel like coming inside and meeting the other guests?"

"Of course, I will greet the rest of the party. I just need to stretch my darn leg. By the time we reach the others I should be right as rain." She gingerly made her way up the steps with Sir Edward's assistance.

"Shall we?" Lord Millington held out his arm to Emma. "I hope Lady Sophia's prattle on the journey hasn't given you the headache?"

She pursed her lips with aversion and frowned before replying, "Thankfully, with a few terse replies to her attempts to discuss the latest fashions and my obvious considerable interest in hearing about Mrs. Wilcox's daily life, she kept quiet most of the journey."

He grimaced. "You noticed I bore the brunt of her ludicrous comments on the final portion of the trip?"

She couldn't stop herself from grinning. "I would say that is a just punishment. You were the one who decided I needed to make friends with a silly, self-absorbed lady who could easily bring immeasurable torment upon me, after hearing her inane babble for hours inside a closed carriage."

"I sincerely apologize for not thinking of the possibility when I made the offer." He paused at the top of the steps where an elderly man with a crown of white hair stood at rigid attention. "Parley; it is good to see you."

The man bowed deeply and then stood tall once more. "Welcome back to Horsham House, my lord."

Lord Millington drew her forward. "This is Lady Emma Brenham."

"Welcome, Lady Emma." The butler bowed to her.

"Parley has been here since I visited as a boy. Edward and I kept him on his toes. We were typical rambunctious lads," Lord Millington explained, with a smile. "He worked his way up from assistant gardener to the exalted position of butler. How many years are you in charge now, Parley?"

"Almost fourteen years, my lord. May I escort you to the drawing room? The others arrived and all except Lady Sophia have gathered."

"We will see ourselves there." Lord Millington put his hand at her back, guiding her forward down a wide hallway.

She stopped to admire a large vase filled with flowers. "How beautiful; the gardens must be extensive."

"They are quite wonderful." He pulled her close to his side and whispered, "I look forward to spending time in them with you."

She frowned, moving away from him as her treasonous heart began to race in reaction to his words. How many other women were told the same thing by him in similar circumstances?

"Is there something wrong?" he asked.

"No, no." She took a deep breath, vowing to enjoy herself and not become preoccupied with concern over Lord Millington's flirtatious tendencies. "I imagine I am a little apprehensive about meeting the others."

"I am sure they will be a friendly group," he assured her. "Lady Sophia still hasn't come down? What can be keeping her?"

She attempted to keep the exasperation out of her voice, without success. "Surely you cannot be surprised at her continued absence? She certainly believes it is in her best interest to make a grand entrance, even at something as casual as a house party in the country."

He pursed his full lips together and sighed. "I am sorry. I encountered many simpering, shy young ladies over the years as well as forward, experienced young widows. I cannot recall meeting anyone quite like her."

She studied him intently. "I am confused. You are saying you were spared the company of an excessively vain woman? How fortunate for you! While thankfully not a common trait, I can think of several ladies who have that unfortunate mannerism and use it with a vengeance."

He smiled down at her. "You are adorable when you pretend to be affronted by my observations."

She stared into his twinkling blue eyes before replying, somewhat breathlessly, "Who said I pretended?"

"A direct hit!" He chuckled as he guided her toward an open doorway to the left of the hallway. The sounds of raised voices and exuberant laughter greeted them as they crossed the threshold.

She observed Sir Edward and an elderly, rather stylish gentleman occupied with helping Mrs. Wilcox into a seat near the fireplace. A tall lady dressed in an elegant day gown showing off her trim figure, with black hair intertwined with streaks of gray, stood close to the door. The woman looked over at them with piercing green eyes as they came into the room. She walked up to them.

"Lucas! I am so happy you could join our party." The elegant lady reached out to touch his arm.

"I am very glad to be here." He bowed and kissed the woman's cheek before turning to Emma. "I want you to meet Lady Emma Brenham. Lady Emma, this is Edward's mother, Lady Margaret Collins."

She curtsied to her hostess. "How do you do, Lady Collins? Thank you so much for including me in your invitation."

"I am pleased you could join us, Lady Emma." She smiled warmly. "Your mother, Therese; I was acquainted with her. Our first London Season occurred in the same year."

Her cheeks grew warm at the pleasure of meeting someone who spent time with her mother. "As you are aware, she died from complications during my birth. If you could find the opportunity, I would enjoy hearing anything you can remember about her."

"I would be happy to speak to you of her. But please, come and meet the others. Here, by your friend, Mrs. Wilcox, is Lord Clifton Topley. Lord Topley, meet Lady Emma Brenham and Lord Millington."

The gentleman broke off his conversation with Mrs. Wilcox as they approached. He stood straight and tall before bowing deeply at the waist, a ruggedly handsome, older man who had certainly aged well. Emma took a moment to notice his cravat tied flawlessly in the classical, Collier de Cheval style. "It is a pleasure to meet you both. I understand you are a particular friend of this woman from the United States, Lady Emma."

She smiled at him. "Yes, I am, Lord Topley. I must confess to an unquenchable curiosity for details about her country. I fear I exhaust her with my queries."

"Nonsense!" Mrs. Wilcox spoke out from the chair. "It pleases me to comprehend you are interested."

Lord Topley chuckled. "I think we are both guilty of that. I have been doing the same thing since we were introduced a few minutes ago."

She joined in the general laughter and then followed Lady Collins to the group of young people standing together in the center of the room where she performed the other introductions.

"Everyone, please meet Lady Emma Brenham and Lord Millington," Lady Collins called out. "This is Mr. Henry Stanhope, son of Viscount Preen. Here is Miss Ellen Cather, daughter of Sir Paul and Lady Ann Cather. Next to her is Frederick Melter, Lord Surd, son of the Earl and Countess of Gladden. Standing next to his right is my daughter, Edward's sister, Miss Camille Collins. And last but by no means least; meet Mr. John Rudder, son of Viscount Tilbrook."

While she acknowledged the introductions, Emma studied each person in turn. Mr. Stanhope had a thatch of red hair covering the top of his head and a short, stocky frame. He sported a pale complexion with a smattering of freckles across his nose and cheek bones. Miss Cather, almost as tall as Emma, had a wealth of blond hair caught up in a complex bun on the crown of her head. Her soft, almost angelic features were complemented by pale blue eyes, a tiny nose, and perfect bow-shaped lips. Lord Surd was of average height. He had corn-colored hair, brushed off his forehead, worn long with the thick strands brushing against his shirt collar. He patted Mr. Stanhope on the back and offered his handkerchief with a grin as Mr. Stanhope attempted to hold back a sneeze.

Miss Collins displayed the same thick, raven-colored hair as her mother and brother. She had a diminutive frame. Her dark locks were braided and wrapped in a long coil around her head. She had inherited the vivid green eyes as well. At present, her orbs were glowing, and a wide smile curved her full lips as she laughed at something Lord Surd said to her. Mr. Rudder proved to be by far the most handsome gentleman in the group; tall and muscular with wavy brown locks sweeping down across one side of his face. His rugged countenance was complimented by a commanding, aristocratic nose, and a deep cleft in his chin.

Greetings were exchanged and Lord Surd had inquired as to their comfort on the journey when the door behind Emma opened with a flourish.

"Lady Sophia Hampton!" Parley announced in a booming voice.

The woman who glided into the doorway, pausing for effect on the threshold, could not be compared to the nitwitted, cranky lady who occupied a seat in the same carriage as Emma a short time ago. Lady Sophia had changed into a bright pink muslin gown with long, tapered sleeves, a triple fall of lace at her throat and an intricate band of Rouleau trim along the edge of the skirt. Emma remembered the lady's earlier lament regarding the plain gowns she brought to the party. If this proved to be her notion of what constituted an austere garment, she feared she would be woefully underdressed.

"Sophia wouldn't settle for anything other than a grand entrance. Her talents were wasted at our finishing school," Miss Collins whispered to Emma as she watched her friend's performance.

"I am sorry to keep all of you waiting." Lady Sophia's thick, black hair was swept up high on the crown of her head in a large pearl-encrusted comb. It shined and twinkled as beams of candlelight reflected off its surface. She slowly moved into the room, pausing a moment in an obvious ploy to make certain to garner everyone's attention, before strolling toward Mrs. Wilcox.

That lady gripped her cane as she stared up at her charge for several moments without speaking. "Did you meet our host and hostess?" she eventually inquired in a curt manner.

"Yes, of course. Sir Edward. We met briefly in the entryway." Lady Sophia gave him her gloved hand and he bowed over it.

He stepped back, studying her. "I must admit to skepticism about the amount of 'damage' you suffered on the journey. A transformation has certainly been made in a relatively short period of time. This is my mother, Lady Collins."

"It is a pleasure." She nodded her head at their hostess in a regal manner. "Thank you for your complimentary words, Sir Edward. It is particularly important I appear my best at all public gatherings."

"Then put your best foot forward and greet this gentleman," Mrs. Wilcox prompted in a no-nonsense tone. "Lord Clifton Topley, this is Lady Sophia, daughter of my good friends Lord and Lady Breech."

The door suddenly opened again. Parley strode inside. "Sir Raeford Crumby!"

Chapter Seventeen

"Who?" Lady Collins frowned at her butler.

"Um…I neglected to inform you…" Lady Sophia's creamy white cheeks turned rosy. "He…He is my particular friend. I invited him for moral support."

"Sophia!" Mrs. Wilcox gasped. "How could you? I sincerely apologize, Lady Collins."

"The numbers will be off." Their hostess reached out to grip the back of a nearby chair.

Parley cleared his throat. "Cook laid out a substantial tea in the dining room, my lady."

Sir Edward stepped forward, taking his mother's arm. "We can sort everything out later. I am certain everyone is famished after their journeys here."

The guests made their way to the door. Lucas studied the most recent, uninvited addition to the party from his spot in the corner of the room. Sir Raeford was of medium height and thin as a reed. That didn't stop him from wearing his shirt points impossibly high and sporting a flamboyant purple waistcoat decorated with silver thread embroidered in the shape of a peacock. A stark contrast to his slim frame, his hair was thick and brown, brushed back off his high forehead to fall with a broad sweep against his collar. Lucas suddenly remembered meeting the gentleman at the Seating ball. He had rarely left Lady Sophia's side at that event. She took the man's arm now, blithely announcing her intention to drink a cup of tea. They preceded Mrs. Wilcox and Lord Topley, who followed at the rear of the group. Lucas heard their conversation as they passed by.

"What were you thinking?" Mrs. Wilcox's voice trembled with anger as she spoke to Lady Sophia's back. "This is not your party."

"Sir Raeford greatly admires me." Lady Sophia paused in the doorway. "It is important he attend."

Her narrow-minded answer certainly deserved no reply. Mrs. Wilcox only shook her head, leaning on her cane as she went out the door.

Lucas noticed Lady Emma studying a painting on the wall near the window. He strolled across the room to stand at her side. "Are you not hungry?"

She turned to look at him, her hands clenched at her side, the irises at the center of her brown eyes smoldering like golden embers, her face flushed. "I needed a moment…I am embarrassed and utterly furious."

Not hard to guess the source of her irritation. "Lady Sophia?"

"Need you ask? Oh, can you believe the unmitigated gall of the woman!" Her voice was low and raspy, laced with notes of fury.

"You need some fresh air." He bent over and whispered in her ear, "I believe most everyone will plan to stay indoors after tea. Would you care to stroll in the garden with me after we finish our repast? Remember, we have a couple of interrupted discussions to complete."

She arched her brows. "I had forgotten. I would appreciate a tour of the outside property."

Her indifferent reply confused him. "You are loath to continue our discourse?"

She looked down at the carpeted floor, frowning before meeting his gaze once more. "No. I confess I find it hard to believe you wish to talk about such mundane matters with me."

"I would hardly call the topics of love and marriage as well as details of how I manage my estate mundane," he retorted. "You are a mature, level-headed woman. I value your opinion and I enjoy talking to you."

"I suppose you expect me to be flattered by your words. Isn't that a compliment on my advanced years?"

He frowned at her, puzzled by her brusque manner. "Not at all. Your age has nothing to do with the fact that I look forward to our discussions. You come across as intelligent and thoughtful when you speak. I am comfortable talking to you."

"Mother sent me to make sure you two weren't lost." Miss Collins walked into the room. "Cook made the most delightful cakes to go with our tea."

"We were just coming," declared Lady Emma, moving away from him, making a beeline for the door. "I am decidedly parched."

Lucas strolled behind the two women, contemplating Lady Emma's obvious hesitation to speak with him. Did he come off so shallow? She mentioned his reputation previously. Was it possible for him to be reputed only for chasing light-skirts and his expertise in bedding them? A sobering factor to contemplate. If that was the case, no wonder she found it difficult to take him seriously. He absentmindedly walked into the dining room, filling his plate with various morsels, before sitting down next to Miss Cather.

He sipped his tea and chewed on the food without tasting it. He listened to Lord Surd, who sat on the other side of Miss Cather, describe one of his horses coming up lame at the start of his journey to Horsham House. At the end of the table, Edward reassured Mrs. Wilcox. He had his hand on her forearm, and he spoke softly with a gentle smile on his face. Across the table, Sir Raeford laughed in a strident manner as he finished telling Lady Sophia some tidbit. He obviously believed himself quite witty.

A few minutes later, the others announced a variety of things they planned to occupy themselves with before coming together again for the evening meal. Mr. Stanhope informed them of his intention to read in the library. Lord Topley said he would join him there. Lord Surd challenged Mr. Rudder to a game of billiards. Edward described some estate business he needed to attend to in his study. Lady Collins and Mrs. Wilcox were planning to enjoy a comfortable discussion about the pleasures of travel in the morning room. Sir Raeford declared he was determined to write a bit of poetry in the privacy of his chamber. Miss Collins apprised them Miss Cather and Lady Sophia were to meet in her room. They intended to catch up on important events in each other's lives since they parted company after completing finishing school.

As a general exodus followed, Lucas looked down at his plate, surprised to find it empty. He dropped his serviette onto the table before pushing back his chair, standing up and heading to the drawing room. He walked onto the terrace from the open French doors. He strolled from there down the stairs leading to the garden, stopping to wait for Lady Emma to join him.

"I am sorry I took so long. My maid insisted I wear a shawl. It took some time for me to locate one that went with my dress."

Lucas turned around to see she had changed her traveling dress into a garment with an overskirt and bodice in a soft peach color. The gown was decorated with tiny bunches of flowers in a matching color. She wore a straw bonnet tied underneath her chin with a pink ribbon, her shawl was of cashmere, in a similar shade of pink.

"You look lovely." He held out his arm to her, getting a whiff of her sweet, lemony scent. "Shall we take this path? It follows the edge of the lawn and leads to a small stream just on this side of the woods."

"Yes. It sounds wonderful," she murmured.

He didn't speak for several moments as he navigated the walkway. "I trust everything is to your liking as far as the accommodations here?"

"Oh yes. I have all I require." She clutched his forearm as they stepped over some loose pebbles that were strewn across the path. "My room overlooks the front of the house. It is a very pleasing vista."

"Edward is exceedingly proud of his home." He looked up to study a stand of tall elm trees a short distance away. "He is an enthusiastic gardener as well."

"Does he spend much time here?" She suddenly stopped walking and tugged on her bonnet strings. "These are too tight."

"Here. Let me assist you." He released her arm, reaching for the ribbons, loosening, and gently retying them under her chin. "They are unnecessarily snug. There aren't any strong winds to deal with today."

"I am afraid my maid decided to be a trifle overzealous when she secured my bonnet." She said the words in a timid, shaky tone and then smiled at him.

"Better now?" He studied her beautiful, upturned face. Her plump, ripe-for-kissing lips were just inches away from his mouth. It would be a simple matter to embrace her, with no one at the house likely to observe them.

Her brown eyes suddenly widened as if she read his mind. She quickly turned around, facing away from him. "Y…yes, thank you."

"You are very welcome." His stomach clenched as if he'd been punched, in reaction to her obvious distain when she offered him the cold shoulder. He was momentarily robbed of the ability to breathe. The past ten years of frequent debauchery brought him to this ominous, eye-opening moment. A lovely, intelligent woman of his class wanted nothing to do with him, believing he viewed an embrace as a mere act of flirtation. He sighed in frustration before offering his arm to her once more. "Shall we?"

"I…I inquired how much time Sir Edward spends here," she prompted him in a breathless tone.

He guided them down the pathway, skirting the lush, green lawn. The air was clear and warm, the sunlight golden. "I believe he lives here year-round with the exception of a month or so in the summer at Brighton and a few weeks in London when Parliament is in session. He takes the responsibility of land ownership quite seriously, as I do."

"I am surprised he hasn't married…" She paused. "I apologize. I must sound like your parents."

He chuckled, patting the hand that rested on his arm as he observed a rosy flush appear on her cheeks. "I trust you can begin to understand the pressures we eligible gentlemen are continually faced with?"

She stopped walking and stared at him. "I comprehend a lady is not to mention such a thing, but I prefer to be blunt. Is the reason you made a reputation for yourself as a gentleman who prefers the company of loose women, your own way of making a statement against marriage?"

He frowned as he pondered her question. "I wouldn't be so harsh as to say I am opposed to it. I admit I put off looking for a wife longer than I should. The grim example of my own father and mother's relationship certainly keeps my enthusiasm for the institution at a low point. Also, it is extremely hard to become motivated by the bashful, tongue-tied young misses who are frequently presented to me for consideration as my future viscountess."

She gripped his forearm with her gloved fingers. "You should try putting yourself in their shoes. Contrary to what their mothers would make you believe, most of them are not mentally prepared to be married when they turn seventeen or eighteen. Some might even have feelings for other men who are deemed ineligible by their parents."

He raised his eyebrows, looking down at her in surprise. "I confess I never contemplated the situation from their point of view. I would like to believe that was not because of my own conceit or feelings of self-importance. Rather, I assumed the young ladies would be eager to set up their own households as part of one of the oldest and wealthiest families in England."

"That certainly sweetens the prize," she agreed.

"I am nothing more than some young lady's bounty then?" he sighed.

"In society's eyes you are a catch, and the first

young lady you offer for would be foolish to turn you down," she countered.

He chuckled, his churlish disposition substantially improved by her gracious comment. "Thank you for your good opinion."

"We have been acquainted long enough, Lord Millington. You must realize I never mince my words," she replied, with a smile.

"As I mentioned before, you are refreshingly honest and direct," he reminded her, absentmindedly stroking her gloved hand. "Don't you want children of your own? I have seen how much you love your nephews. I also observed the look of longing in your eyes when you pointed out the little girl to us in town the other day."

"Not at the expense of gaining an indifferent husband. Obviously, I am no authority on marriage. I am twenty-five, never betrothed. I have no knowledge of the emotion called love. I am considered to be past my prime and 'on the shelf'." She frowned before taking a deep breath. "I would like to believe I held out for happiness. I am not willing to wed a well-heeled, drunken lord simply to avoid being called an ape-leader or an old maid. My vision of the perfect family life is one where both parents spend time with their children on a daily basis. What about you, Lord Millington, what would make you happy and content?"

He pondered his answer for a moment. "A few weeks ago, I would have told you I want to be free. Free to spend time on my estate, free to travel to London when I get the urge to mingle in society, spend time at my club. My father and mother are correct when they advise me it is past time to provide an heir to ensure the family succession. Recently, I have had several vague dreams where I see a lovely woman sitting in the garden at my estate surrounded by a cluster of laughing children. I deliberated how wonderful it would be to have a happy, devoted marriage to serve as an opposite example to my parents' miserable existence."

"Forgive me, but I find it impossible to believe what you say," she told him, in a harsh tone, releasing him. "Are you attempting to impress me?"

Her bitter inflection surprised him until he recalled her misconstrued opinion of his character. It was an exercise in futility to believe she would blithely accept his last statements. He replied, somberly, "I assure you. I speak sincerely."

"We find ourselves at an impasse then," she sighed, turning away from him.

Perhaps a change of scene would improve her perspective. He studied the pathway. "I believe there is a bench around the corner on the other side of the hedge. It is close to the stream. Would you like to sit down?"

"Yes, of course," she murmured.

He offered her his arm again. "It is around this way."

They followed the path as it curved at the edge of the lawn; a tall, semi-circle shrub surrounding a rustic, wooden bench. The spot hid from view anyone who might be looking at the garden from inside the house. Leaves on the nearby elm trees rustled softly in the light breeze. Birds chirped and a stream leading from a small, nearby lake babbled softly as water flowed across the pebbles; a private, idyllic setting on a warm, summer afternoon.

"It is lovely here." She let go of his arm and settled herself on the far end of the bench. "Are the gardens at your estate anything like this? Is it close by?"

He strolled forward, placing one booted foot on the bench. He rested one elbow on his knee as he leaned over, cupping his chin in his hand. "It is a few hours ride from here; in the town of Bucklebury, Berkshire. The area surrounding my property is not as wooded as this is; the main lawn is smaller, but I do own a large rose garden."

"I imagine there are several people employed to take care of it for you?"

"No, as a matter of fact, I have only one gardener," he refuted. "You remember I mentioned previously, I do reside part of the year at my estate? I enjoy spending time outdoors. I often potter in my garden."

Her brown eyes widened, and she gasped. "I…I confess I believed you were jesting about visiting your property. How frequently are you there?"

"At least once a month for several days," he acknowledged with a grin. "Do I shock you?"

Her cheeks flushed, and she looked away from him. "I…I envisioned the life of a full-fledged rake would require all your attention."

"Ah, yes, there is the matter of my renowned reputation." He sighed and then frowned down at her bent head. He dropped his foot to the ground, standing up. He reached out, gently caressing the tip of her chin with his fingers until she moved to stare up at him; her brown eyes glistening with unshed tears. "I fear I must astonish you even further by admitting I give very little consideration to that aspect of my life."

She didn't speak for a moment; simply looking up at him before coming to her feet, reaching out for him. "Did I misjudge you?"

"No. I wouldn't say that. And you would heartily

agree if you could read my mind at this moment." He dropped his hand, stepping away from her. "I blame myself. It was not a good plan to escort you out here away from the others. In a matter of moments, I will be kissing those luscious lips of yours. I would never forgive myself if I compromised you. I must go. I will see you at dinner."

Chapter Eighteen

Emma spooned some egg into her mouth and then took a bite of her toast. Lord Millington sat across the table from her. She kept her eyes lowered, not wanting to encounter his frank, questioning look. The incident in the garden had left her shaken. After their discussion yesterday, she realized her assumptions about him were misguided. Thankfully, she sat between Lady Sophia and Mr. Stanhope at dinner the night before. Other than a few comments about the Prince Regent's excessive expenses at Brighton and high price of lodgings in London, Mr. Stanhope applied himself to his food. Even in more settled situations, Emma knew it was pointless to attempt anything other than a murmured agreement to whatever subject Lady Sophia happened to be expounding upon. As soon as their hostess stood up, indicating the meal had concluded and the ladies should retire to the drawing room, Emma escaped to her bedchamber, pleading a headache.

She had tossed and turned in her bed before falling asleep just after dawn. She dreamed of Lord Millington. He kissed her. She remembered straining toward him, pressing her trembling lips against his, wanting more of the warm, tingly sensations caressing her body at his intimate touch. At present, with that gentleman in such close proximity, Emma found herself reliving the dream. She needed to wipe the image from her mind and avoid speaking to him until she regained her equilibrium.

Lady Collins took a sip of her tea from her place at the foot of the table and wiped her serviette across her mouth. "I wish to inform all of you I obtained the musical services of a local duo for this afternoon. Since we keep country hours, I thought it would be nice to provide the opportunity for some dancing before dinner tonight. What did you plan for this morning, Camille?"

"The weather is lovely, not too warm. The ladies could challenge the gentlemen to a game of shuttlecock." She grinned as choruses of cheers as well as groans were heard from the others at the table. "Come on! It will be fun! There are plenty of battledores to go around."

"How do you normally play?" Lord Surd questioned with eager interest. "Do you add points for every hit? Or do you start with a certain amount and subtract for every miss?"

"I prefer starting with twenty points," Miss Collins explained. "We could begin with four people, two on each side. A point is lost for each missed hit after the initial contact with the battledore is made. We rotate teams after one side loses all their points or after a suitable amount of time passes if both teams stay even."

"Unless the court is underneath a large, shady tree, you understand I cannot play, Camille." Lady Sophia stretched her neck, thrusting her chin outward. "My fine complexion, you see. I never subject myself to direct sunlight."

"I am certain such a rambunctious game wouldn't be conducive to someone who suffered a headache last evening either," Lord Millington spoke up. "Perhaps Lady Emma and Lady Sophia would like to join me and Edward for a game of billiards."

"That is a capital idea." Sir Edward took a sip of coffee.

Emma frowned at Lord Millington. "I am sorry, but it wouldn't be much of a challenge for you. I never played the game."

"I will gladly show you the ropes." He grinned at her. "We could play in teams; you and me against Edward and Lady Sophia."

"Have you ever played, Lady Sophia?" Sir Edward asked.

"I attempted it. My uncle, who resides in London, has a table. He taught my cousin and me how to play several years ago," she replied. "I shall need to be shown how to hold the cue again."

"We are evenly matched then," Lord Millington observed. "Edward is not as good as I am, but Lady Sophia has played before."

Sir Edward choked on his coffee. "I beg to differ. I am certainly the better billiards player."

"We shall see." Lord Millington chuckled. "Is it decided then? Lady Emma, Lady Sophia, will you both join us?"

"We will be fine with three people on each of our teams. We can rotate if need be," clarified Miss Collins. She looked around the room with a frown. "Where is Sir Raeford?"

"He told me last night he never appears in public before two o'clock in the afternoon," Lady Sophia informed her. "And then he only makes an appearance because he is hungry."

Miss Collins raised her brows. "Is that so? Well, we won't concern ourselves over his entertainment. Mother, will you join us?"

"Of course. But first, I need to inform Cook to provide a substantial tea this afternoon," declared Lady Collins.

Sir Edward smiled at his mother. "That would be advisable. I am certain we will all be famished after the morning's activities."

"And Sir Raeford will be hungry after sleeping the day away," Lady Collins countered, with obvious sarcasm. "Lord Topley and Mrs. Wilcox, do you wish to stay inside today?"

Lord Topley wiped his mouth on his serviette. "Mrs. Wilcox has agreed to join me for a leisurely stroll by the lake."

"Yes. I am quite anxious to see more of the grounds," Mrs. Wilcox related, with a smile. "I had a glimpse of some trees and a bit of blue water from inside the house."

Lord Surd pushed his chair back from the table and stood up. "Should the shuttlecock players meet outside in a few minutes?"

"Yes, meet me by the shed at the back of the house near the kitchen garden," Miss Collins advised. "That is where the outdoor game equipment is stored."

The others made haste to finish their meal. After taking a final sip of their tea or coffee, most exited the room. Emma slowly stood up.

"I trust I'm not being presumptuous in assuming you would prefer to stay indoors today." Lord Millington walked up to her side, offering her his arm. "I also comprehend what a trial Lady Sophia can be."

"I resigned myself to tolerating her company for the remainder of our stay here," Emma answered. "Perhaps I am refining too much on her character. After all, your parents appear to believe she would make you a good wife."

"That is a perfect illustration of why my father and mother are not authorities on what makes a happy marriage," he uttered, with a grimace. "I would rather talk about you."

"Me?" The change of subject caught her off guard.

"Yes, you, Lady Emma, so lovely, sweet, and intelligent." He smiled at her. "Did I embarrass you in the garden yesterday? Is that the reason you avoided speaking to me last night at dinner and then claimed to suffer from a bad head later in the evening?"

"No, no!" She considered prevaricating but changed her mind. "I wouldn't describe it as embarrassment, rather the situation made me feel awkward and somewhat perplexed."

His smile disappeared and he frowned at her. "I am sorry. I never intended that to happen. I needed to leave before I did something distasteful to you."

"Distasteful?" She did not understand his word choice. "Although, my common sense would surely revert itself afterward, a kiss from you would never, ever be undesirable to me."

His eyebrows rose and he chuckled. "Well then, I am vexed I let the opportunity pass by."

She smiled up at him, suddenly feeling brazen. "I am hopeful there will be another chance."

****

"Indeed? I'll see what I can contrive, then." Lucas grinned at her. "Shall we make our way to the billiards' room?"

They walked down the hall together. The door to the game room stood open. He stopped, extending his free hand out in front of him, sanctioning her to enter first.

"There you are!" Edward bent over the billiard table racking up the balls. "Lady Sophia will be down soon. Why don't you show Lady Emma how to hold a cue stick, Lucas?"

"With pleasure." He walked over to the rack of various sized sticks on the wall and then turned to study her. "You are tall, but your arms are of average length. We'll give this one a try."

She walked over to a chair, dropping her shawl onto the seat before joining him. "What exactly determines if it is a good fit?"

"The point of the stick needs to be long enough to reach at least halfway across when you are leaning over the table to make a shot," he explained. "Come over here. I'll stand behind you. Hold it with your right hand about four inches from the end."

She stepped in front of him and took the stick. "Now what?"

"With your left hand, form a letter O using your thumb and forefinger, like so." He held up his hand to illustrate. "Put the tip of the stick through that O, grip the end of the stick with your right hand and you're ready to shoot."

"Here is a cue ball." Edward rolled the white ball down toward them and then removed the rack from the other balls.

"Did you start without me?" Lady Sophia strolled into the room. "My hair needed to be centered correctly on the crown of my head. I asked my maid to fix it."

"No, we haven't begun to play yet," Edward told her. "Lady Emma is getting a lesson on how to hold a cue stick."

"You must show me as well," Lady Sophia commanded, as she dropped her shawl and gloves on the cushion of an overstuffed loveseat in the corner of the room.

"Come over here, then." Edward studied the other cue sticks.

"I am going to help Lady Emma try a few shots to get the feel for the most advantageous maneuvers," Lucas informed Edward.

"Go ahead. Here is an extra cue ball." Edward picked out a stick, waving Lady Sophia over to his side. "We will practice over here."

Lucas gathered a couple of solid-colored balls and rolled them toward his partner. When they came to a stop in front of her, he moved back into position behind her. "Now, lean over like this. Take your right hand, aim the point of the stick at the white cue ball and push it through the O in your left hand so the white ball hits the colored ball. Ideally, the colored ball will drop into a pocket."

"Like this?" She jerked her right hand forward and the cue stick sailed over the top of the intended ball.

"Not exactly; let me show you." He moved closer, bracing his left arm on the edge of the table, just brushing against her waist as he leaned over her. Her hair smelled lovely, of roses and lemon. Momentarily distracted, he told himself to concentrate on the matter in front of him, not mooning over the fragrance of a lady's hair. He covered her right hand with his own, moving the cue stick forward with a smooth, even motion. The cue ball rolled into the colored one and stopped.

"It didn't get to the pocket." She chuckled as she stated the obvious.

Although he thoroughly enjoyed the sensation of

bending over Lady Emma's backside, he admonished himself to recall the role he should be playing. He pictured chunks of ice floating on a lake in order to temper the bulge currently forming in the front of his breeches before resuming the lesson. "Ah, yes. You need a bit more momentum in your thrust. When the balls are touching like that, it is called kissing."

"Very interesting. We can't get away from that subject today, can we?" she turned in his arms, smiling up at him.

He couldn't resist her sudden, flirtatious demeanor. He leaned over to whisper in her ear, the silken strands of her hair tickling his chin. "If we were alone, it would be more than just a word, I can assure you."

Her brown eyes widened. "How…how unfortunate, another missed opportunity."

"Are you two quite ready?" Edward called from the other end of the table.

"I am thinking we should play Eight Ball?" asked Lady Sophia, with a toss of her head.

"You comprehend more about this game than I believed." Edward grinned at her. "Solids and Stripes would be easier."

"I suppose. If you insist," she answered, with a sigh.

Lucas took a deep breath as he stepped away from Lady Emma. He looked at her with eyebrows raised. "Are you prepared to try this?"

"Yes. I will do the best I can."

"That is all anyone can ask; give the contest a sporting try." He turned toward Edward, who was busy racking up the balls. "Did we decide on Eight Ball or Solids and Stripes?"

"We will play Solids and Stripes first," he said.

"Then the ladies can decide if they want to continue."

"Good enough." Lucas positioned the cue ball in front of the racked balls. "Shall I break?"

"This is my favorite part." Lady Sophia leaned over the table, clutching her cue stick in her hand. "I love to watch a big, strong man scatter the balls across the hard surface."

Edward laughed. "How is it that you can make a simple comment sound so bawdy?"

"Keep your mind on the game if you want to win, man," Lucas advised, with a chuckle as he hit the white cue ball with the tip of his stick. It rebounded with a loud clack against the group of colored balls. A striped one fell into the far corner pocket.

"Did you see that?" Edward called out, looking at Lady Sophia. "We are solids."

Lucas moved to the other side of the table, aiming toward another striped ball. This time he missed. He strolled over to Lady Emma's side as Edward studied the ball placement. "You probably understand the essence of the game. We need to get all the striped balls in the pockets first in order to win."

"Yes. I gathered that."

Edward turned to Lady Sophia. "There aren't many open shots. Do you want me to go first?"

"I think that would be wise," she assented.

Lucas bent over to whisper in his partner's ear. "We'll soon see how well Edward is playing today."

"He did claim to be the one with the most talent," she reminded him. "I am impressed with your first hit. Did you call it breaking?"

"Yes," he answered. "You could also call it a breach of the racked balls."

"I got one!" Edward called out. "And there goes another one."

"You often start out strong and then fade as the game goes on," Lucas teased as Edward bent over the table to shoot again.

"Oh, you missed!" Lady Sophia pouted as the ball bounced off one side. "I hope I have an opportunity for an easy shot."

"Wait and see how your other opponent performs," Lucas told her before turning to Lady Emma. "Do you need me to suggest a move?"

"No, thank you." She smiled at him before walking up to the table. "This striped ball perched in front of the pocket should be easy."

"Wait." He scowled. "I forgot one of the rules. If the cue ball drops into the pocket after a ball, you lose your turn and both balls are returned to the table."

She turned back to study him. "What would you like me to do?"

He stood next to her, pointing at the cue ball. "I advise you to hit it at an angle. Then you can tap the colored ball into the pocket and the white one will roll to the side."

She frowned. "Perhaps there is another, easier shot?"

He studied the position of the remaining striped balls. "No, there isn't. Go ahead and try it."

"Very well." She bent over the table, putting the tip of the stick through her fingers and tapped the cue ball. It rolled to the striped one, nudging it into the pocket.

"Well done! That shot is extremely hard to make," Lucas told her, hoping to inspire confidence.

"I'm bewildered. Are you certain you never played

before?" Lady Sophia demanded, with a frown.

"This is my first time," Lady Emma assured her.

"Let's see what she can do on the next shot," Edward advised. "This move will be much harder to pull off."

"Um." Lady Emma contemplated her choices. "I will try hitting the red and white striped ball on the other side of the table."

"Yes," Lucas agreed. "That is about all you can do."

She tapped the cue ball with some force. It rolled across the table and hit the intended ball but after moving several inches, it stopped a good way away from the pocket. "Oh, no!"

"You did the best you could," he declared, not wishing her to become discouraged. "It is always hard to strike the cue ball with accuracy when it is sitting so close to the side of the table. There is not much room left to get your shot off cleanly."

"It's my turn!" Lady Sophia lowered her cue stick, getting into position. She tapped the white ball. It rolled back down the table where it connected with a yellow solid one, falling into the nearest pocket.

"Well played!" Edward called out. "Let me see you do that again."

"Do you doubt my abilities?" Lady Sophia frowned at him.

"No, no!" Edward replied, bracingly. "I'm simply thinking of the odds, a beginner sinking two balls in a row."

"Perhaps I will surprise you, then," she answered flirtatiously before leaning over the table, pointing her cue stick at the white ball and striking it. The cue ball struck the blue solid one, but that ball rolled past the intended pocket, coming to a stop in the middle of the table. "What happened?"

"You hit the cue ball straight on and didn't take into account the pocket you were aiming for was positioned to the right side of the ball," Edward explained.

Lucas stepped up to the table, studying the placement of the remaining striped balls. He saw a couple of opportunities for dropping two more. He bent over and made his first shot. The cue ball hit the striped one with a hard smack to the side and it fell into the corner pocket. He turned the other direction, aiming at another striped ball nearby. It rolled up to the pocket but deflected at the last minute by a solid ball partially blocking the opening. "Drat! Not enough spin on that to get around the solid one."

"Better luck next time, my friend," Edward chuckled as he moved forward to make his shot. He dropped the red solid into a pocket before pitching the orange and then the cue ball together into a side pocket. "Damn! Sorry, ladies!"

"You were overeager," Lucas informed him as he strolled around the table to pull the two balls out of the pocket. "You are aware a shot like that requires more finesse."

"What happens now?" Lady Emma asked him from across the table.

"My partner and I are going to discuss strategy," Edward announced as he led Lady Sophia to a far corner of the room. "We will be with you in a minute."

Lucas crooked his finger at Lady Emma. "Come over here and stand next to me."

She walked over, looking up at him with her big brown eyes, licking her lips. "Is it hard?"

Chapter Nineteen

"Uh, what?"

"The next move, after the cue ball goes in the pocket, is it hard?" Emma asked Lord Millington again.

He cleared his throat, before turning back to the table. "Oh, no...no, as a matter of fact, you get an advantage. We roll their ball back out into play again, like so. Then you take the cue ball. Put it behind this mark at the spot you judge is easiest to reach a striped one that is positioned close to another pocket."

"That sounds simple enough," she conceded, as she studied the options. "What would you suggest I do?"

"The green and white striped ball in the far corner," he recommended. "It looks far but it is directly in front of the pocket. Place the cue ball here. Try to hit the ball with some force, on this side. It should roll in, leaving the cue ball in play on the table."

"Are you ready to make your shot?" Edward asked as he and Lady Sophia joined them.

"Yes, we determined what move would be best," Emma responded as she took the cue ball in her hand, taking a position on the opposite corner from where Lord Millington stood.

"Try to keep your shooting hand as steady as you can," he advised. "Give the ball a good whack. It should hit the other ball squarely."

"I will keep that in mind," she replied as she bent

over the table, too late realizing she gave Lord Millington an unimpeded view of her cleavage. She took a deep breath, forcing herself to concentrate on the shot. She moved her right wrist forward, hitting the cue ball with some force. It shot across the table, smacking the striped one before the ball dropped into the pocket. "I did it!"

"Well done!" Lord Millington strolled over to her side. "I couldn't manage it any better."

Lady Sophia sighed from her place at the foot of the table. "I find it hard to believe you never played before."

"Take heart," Sir Edward counseled her. "We came up with a very good plan to win."

"Go ahead. You take another shot," Lord Millington instructed. "I see a couple of possibilities."

She studied the table. "I will attempt getting that ball in the side pocket. I assume I need to gently graze the outer side for it to fall in the other direction?"

He grinned down at her. "Yes, you are correct, but be certain you hit it with enough force to make the ball roll in and not just *kiss* it."

Emma laughed. "That word again!"

"Come on you two," Sir Edward broke in. "We want a chance to show how it's done."

"I am ready." She leaned over the table once more, noting Lord Millington had moved, not looking her way. He studied the ball placement. She quickly flicked her right wrist, tapped the cue ball. It rolled past the striped one to come to a stop a few inches away. "Nothing to show for that move, not even a hug!" she teased.

He stared at her, his intense blue eyes gleaming. "Are you sorry they didn't *kiss?*"

"Most definitely!" she countered with a grin.

It didn't take long for the game to finish. The strategy Sir Edward and Lady Sophia discussed served them well; she dropped one ball in a corner pocket and then missed. He followed her, making all the remaining shots.

"Hard luck, you two," consoled Sir Edward when they were done. "Do you want to play another one?"

Lady Sophia walked over to the sofa to gather her gloves and shawl. "Perhaps another time. I am going to talk to my maid about my gown for the dancing this afternoon and discuss how I want my hair styled."

"Fine." Sir Edward didn't appear surprised by her self-indulgent comments. "My horse needs exercising. I am going to change and go for a short ride. Would you care to join me, Lucas?"

"Give me a few minutes," he replied. "I'll meet you at the stables in a half hour."

"That suits me," Sir Edward answered as he headed for the door. "Good game, Lady Emma."

"Thank you. I enjoyed it. You are a good teacher, Lord Millington." She walked over to the chair, bending over to gather her things. She straightened up, took a step backward, and bumped into his solid chest. "Oh!"

"I want to show you how something else is done," he whispered. "Were you serious when you said you wanted me to kiss you?"

Emma took a deep breath as she turned around to face him. She pondered his question. She greatly appreciated his many kindnesses to her and as well as his compliments. She enjoyed talking to him. He made her feel truly desirable as a woman and not someone to be made fun of because of her large breasts. Could it be wrong to want a kiss from him? "Yes…yes. I meant what

197

I said."

"Very well, then." He moved to stand directly in front of her, his hands resting on her shoulders. "Close your eyes and give me those luscious lips."

She stood on tiptoe, placing her mouth over his. She closed her eyes. The initial heady sensations of the embrace quickly threatened to overwhelm her. Her knees buckled; her shawl dropped unheeded to the floor. She swayed against him, grasping the lapels on his coat with shaking fingers as his lips covered her own.

With his kiss she experienced a fantasy. She knew herself to be as precious as a princess, yet as powerful as a goddess. She reveled in the heady, tingling sensations brought on by his touch; the warmth of his hand at her back, his muscular thigh pressed against her leg. His lips shifted over hers with deliciously unhurried gentleness, teasing her with feathery kisses and tiny pecks upon her mouth until she moaned.

He angled his head, moving closer. Something touched the seam of her lips. She gasped in surprise. Her astonishment turned to fascination as his tongue entered her mouth to begin a sensual dance with her own. Their tongues dueled together. She savored the taste of him, delighting in the riveting emotions coursing throughout her body. She experienced a thrilling sense of power. She alone, in this moment, had garnered his tender, passionate embrace.

He suddenly broke free, making a muffled groaning sound from deep inside his throat. He stared down at her, his blue orbs intense, glowing. "I trust you learned something from this?"

Her breath came out shaky and erratic. For a moment she gripped him, not wanting the embrace to be over. But she quickly decided not to give him clear, unquestionable evidence of her great desire for him. She lowered her hands to her sides, moving away. It took all the fortitude she possessed to not reach out and kiss him again. "Yes, thank you, my lord. A lovely experience I will always remember and treasure."

He started at her words, stepping backward as if she had slapped him. "Indeed?"

"Is it not obvious?" She gave him a wobbly smile, making herself casually bend over to retrieve her shawl. "I am a spinster. I have had little chance to experience such an embrace."

"You make it sound as if I simply bestowed a favor upon you." He frowned at her. "Surely you could tell I enjoyed the experience as well?"

She draped her shawl across her shoulders before answering him. "I'm sorry; I cannot answer your query. If I say yes, it appears I hold an extremely high opinion of my charms. If I say no, then my previous words of praise for your kiss will be turned into a falsehood."

"I see your point," he replied, in a somber tone. "You will favor me with a dance later this afternoon?"

"Yes, of course." She turned away from him and walked to the door. "Enjoy your ride."

****

Lucas' valet helped him quickly change into appropriate riding attire. He made his way to the stables. Edward led his stallion outside. "Just in time," he told him. "The lads are saddling your horse. Here they are now."

"Wonderful." Lucas took the reins from the groom, put his boot in the stirrup and swung his leg over the saddle. "I'm ready."

Edward settled himself on his horse. "Follow me. We will take the trail that goes by the river. It's wide enough to ride abreast. I want to talk to you."

"Should I be concerned?" He grinned as he steered his restive horse behind Edward's.

"No, no. I want to clarify something," Edward called over his shoulder.

Up ahead, there was an open field before they reached the trail. Both men let their horses canter across the meadow so they could stretch their legs.

"What did you want to ask me?" he inquired, as they slowed their horses to a walk when they reached the wider path.

"Do you intend to offer for Lady Sophia?" Edward came to the point without hesitation.

He frowned at the ground. "No. Once again my father and mother will be displeased because I did not do as they asked."

Edward chuckled. "You never took kindly to them ordering you about and telling you how to live your life."

"That is because they consider themselves authorities on what constitutes a proper marriage between men and women in our society," he replied, looking up and spotting Miss Collins, Lord Surd, and Mr. Rudder riding toward them on their own mounts. "In my opinion, their way of life is a dismal substitute for a happy union."

"You are content to leave your situation as it is at present then?" Edward asked. "A confirmed bachelor for the foreseeable future?"

His stomach muscles suddenly clenched before dropping and lurching like a tumultuous hurricane inside his abdomen. Then the air sucked out of his lungs. He struggled to speak. "No…no, not…not at all."

Edward sat up straight in his saddle, staring at him. "What are you saying?"

"I have been a fool!" he shouted. Lucas yanked on the reins turning his horse in the other direction. "I must return to the house. I'll leave you to entertain the others."

Chapter Twenty

"I believe this is my dance, Lady Sophia." Lucas strolled up to a group of chairs thoughtfully placed at the edge of the room. She and Sir Raeford were sitting on two of the seats with their heads together, giggling over some inane observation. Lucas did his best to mingle with the others while he waited for Lady Emma. He had attempted to speak with her after he returned from his ride, but she and Lady Collins were deep in a discussion about her late mother. She joined him as the dancing started but then noticed a torn piece of lace on the bottom edge of her gown. She had gone up to her bedchamber to ask her maid to repair it.

"Lord Millington." Lady Sophia turned to face him. He perceived a half-full champagne glass in her hand. "There has not been much opportunity for us to talk."

"We can rectify that now during the dance." He bowed, offering her his hand.

"Very well." She sighed as she stood up, tossing off the rest of her drink before handing her empty glass to Sir Raeford. "Procure another for me, if you will."

"It would be my pleasure," he replied, before coming to his feet, bowing, and turning to walk out of the room, presumably to carry out her request.

She gave Lucas her hand. He guided her to a spot a short distance away where the carpet had been rolled back to reveal an expanse of wood floor. Music for the evening was provided by the local Vicar's son and daughter; he played the violin exquisitely, while she proved excellent on the pianoforte. At that moment, they struck up a waltz.

Lucas reached out to put his hand on Lady Sophia's waist; she placed her arm on his shoulder. With clasped right and left hands, he led her onto the center of the dance floor.

"It is customary to compliment a lady on her looks, my lord," she informed him, while batting her eyelashes. "Do I displease you in some manner?"

"I'm sorry, very thoughtless of me." He flinched in surprise, realizing other than Lady Emma, he had failed to discern any of the other women in the room. He forced himself to study the lady he danced with. She wore a puce crepe, long-sleeved gown, cut low and square around her bust. Jet beads decorated the bodice. Violet colored crepe roses trimmed the bottom of her skirt. Her hair had been parted across her forehead, allowing the strands to curl in light, loose ringlets around her face. He vaguely recalled her mentioning the gown on their trip to Horsham House. "You look quite beautiful, Lady Sophia."

She pursed her full lips together, staring up at him with her striking violet eyes. "I cannot recall ever being required to request a compliment from a gentleman."

"I apologize for my boorish manners." He spun her around Lord Surd and Miss Collins who were dancing nearby.

"Simple regrets are not enough. You are under an obligation to console and comfort me," she censured him. Her lips suddenly formed an O. "*Hiccup!*"

He stopped dancing. "How many glasses of

champagne did you drink?"

She frowned and pondered his query. "Uh, three or four, I didn't count. Champagne has nothing to do with our discussion."

"It has everything to do with it," he informed her, with a direct, severe tone. "I now comprehend why you were not making any sense."

"Men like you need to be shown, not told," she retorted, before reaching up with both of her hands to pull him toward her. She kissed him on the lips.

He shook her hands off his shoulders, stepping away. As he did so, he saw a movement out of the corner of his eye. He pivoted. Lady Emma stood at the edge of the dance floor with her hand over her mouth. A tear rolled down her cheek just before she spun around and ran from the room.

"No!" he cried out.

"We haven't finished our dance!" Lady Sophia shrieked at him.

Lucas ignored her. He leaped across the floor to the hallway in the direction he imagined Lady Emma was headed. The door to the library stood ajar; his hunch must have been correct! He sighed with relief and strode forward ready to give Emma a concise explanation of what had happened, but the room was empty.

He sprinted out into the hall once more, studying the closed doors that confronted him. Perhaps she had gone toward the entry. He strode down the hallway, hailing Parley. "Did Lady Emma pass by you recently?"

"No, my lord." He bowed. "She hasn't been here."

He deliberated the possibilities. There was a chance she had entered the drawing room. Lucas turned, marching purposefully toward the chamber. He reached the door, grasped the knob before yanking it open and striding into the chamber. Edward sat by the fire drinking a glass of brandy.

"Have you seen...?"

"Lord Millington! I need your help!" Mrs. Wilcox limped into the room behind him.

Lucas turned to her. "What is wrong?"

"I saw Emma go outside. I called to her, but she did not hear me. I followed her, doing my poor best to keep up. When I reached the lawn, she wasn't there. But I did find this." She lifted her hand. She clutched a battered, torn piece of cloth. "It is from her gown."

A ringing started in Lucas' ears, and his heart pounded erratically. He forced himself to take a deep breath and concentrate. He took the material from her quivering fingers. "Where did you find it?"

She pursed her shaking lips together before replying, "I...I pulled it off the bottom of an open gate leading into the woods."

Edward put down his glass, standing up and making his way across the room to join them. "The gate leads to a little-used pathway at the edge of the property. The vegetation on the other side is nothing but tangled tree limbs, half-dead shrubs, and coarse, rocky ground. Why would she go walking there?"

"I believe I am at fault," Lucas replied, in a bleak tone. "Lady Emma saw something she has misinterpreted."

Mrs. Wilcox clutched her cane before uttering, "Surely she cannot go far in her flimsy slippers."

"I will find her," Lucas vowed, as he moved to the door. "Do not worry."

"I am coming as well." Edward followed close

behind him.

****

"I trust Emma won't think it presumptuous of us to stop at Horsham House and tell her the news?" Celia pulled on her handkerchief with a trembling hand, looking up at her husband sitting next to her in the carriage.

"Besides obviously being happy for her, she will be grateful to hear of your aunt's marriage. We were all concerned after not receiving a letter from her for several weeks." He patted his wife's arm. "After all, Emma will need to begin looking for a companion to reside with her at her home in London without delay."

Celia sighed as she studied her two sons sitting on the opposite seat. Miraculously, they were both quiet. Evan read a book and Nicholas stared out of the window. "I wish Emma would get married. I am aware she longs for a family of her own."

"You also know Emma will only marry for love, something you and I can highly recommend doing," he replied with a smile.

"That man is carrying a dog in his bag!" Nicholas sat up, pressing his nose to the window, clutching the sill. "I think it is trying to escape!"

"Let me see." Evan dropped his book, peering over his brother's shoulder. "That is too big to be a dog and it has two…It is a woman! Father, stop the carriage! We must save her!"

"What?" Vernon turned in his seat, looking out of the window. Just to the side of the carriage, he observed a vaguely familiar man, struggling to maintain his grip on a large parcel while frantically kicking his horse's flanks, compelling the mare forward. "Sir Charles?"

Celia clutched his arm. "Oh no! He has captured Emma!"

Vernon rapped on the carriage roof. "James! Stop at once!"

****

Lucas emerged from the house with Edward on his heels. "Would it be faster to enter the wood from the road?"

"Yes. Come this way." Edward sprinted around the edge of the stone wall bordering the main drive.

Lucas ran behind him scanning the surrounding area for any sign of Emma. Perhaps she made her way out of the dense forest and came around to the front of the house. He still clutched the torn piece of fabric from her dress in his hand. He stuffed it inside his coat pocket. *He must find her!*

"There is a carriage pulled over to the side of the road!" Edward shouted.

They both rushed forward toward the vehicle. Suddenly, the door on the carriage burst open. Two young lads, tripping over themselves in their haste, emerged, jumping to the ground. "Hurry, Father! We might be too late!"

"What the…?" Lucas ran toward the carriage just as Vernon emerged.

"I saw Sir Charles ride by. He headed into the woods." Vernon pointed. "You can see the broken branch there. A large sack was draped over the front of his saddle. The boys saw something move inside of it."

"Nicholas believed it to be a dog," clarified Evan. "But the thing is a woman. There were two round…"

"That is enough, Evan," his father said in a steadfast tone. "We are certainly grateful for your keen observations."

"How long would it take to unhitch one of the horses?" Edward asked.

"Too much time," Lucas answered. "I am going to track him down on foot."

"I will come too," Vernon said.

"No." Lucas's firm answer stopped any further argument. "She is my responsibility now. I intend to make a formal request for her hand when this is over."

Vernon slapped him on the back. "Good. Bring her back safe."

"I will," Lucas promised.

Celia frowned as she stood gripping the carriage door. "But Sir Charles is on a horse. He will surely get away."

"He is on an unmarked trail in dense brush, contending with a struggling woman. He won't get far. I will see she is unharmed; I give you my pledge on that, Lady Dentley." Lucas turned away, racing up the slope leading to the woods as if a hundred mad dogs were at his heels.

"I will go after him to make sure they can find their way back," Edward called to the others as he followed him.

Lucas scaled the hill, pausing at the top to look around. It quickly became apparent Sir Charles intended to forge his own path through the tangled vines and prickly shrubs choking the landscape. His trail proved easy to spot, littered with broken branches and crushed plants. Lucas pushed forward through the labyrinth of dense undergrowth, pausing for a moment when he noticed a dark red stain on the pointed tip of a limb. He cursed, shoving a broken chunk of tree trunk away with the bottom of his boot while, at the same time, sending up a silent plea for Emma's safety.

He leapt around a particularly nasty-looking gorse bush to find himself in a small clearing. Up ahead, he spotted his quarry. Sir Charles sat in the saddle of a hapless, aged mare. A large sack was propped up in front of him, draped across the horse's back. Lucas sighed with relief when he noticed movement inside the bag, certain proof Emma remained conscious, but he quickly became concerned. He had left the house without securing a weapon. It would be foolhardy to make him aware of his presence before trying to determine if Sir Charles carried a gun. Forcing himself to remain as quiet as possible, he dropped down behind the bush.

"Will you cease your struggles? You made me poke myself on a branch," sweating, red-faced Sir Charles grumbled as he gripped the bag with one hand, pulling on the reins with the other. "You won't get away. My coach is waiting on the other side of this hill."

Lucas saw and heard enough. Sir Charles literally had his hands full. He needed to make his move. He must get the blackguard to release the sack while at the same time, catch hold of it before it fell to the ground. If that were to occur, Emma could be gravely injured.

"Do you need my assistance?" Edward's voice sounded in his ear.

"Can you drag him away from the horse? I'll be a distraction and get him off-balance. Once he is down, you can deal with him while I take care of Emma."

"I understand," Edward acknowledged.

He slipped out from behind the bush with Edward following closely. Keeping one eye on the bulging bag, he darted up to the horse.

"Not so fast!" Lucas yelled as he grabbed the man's boot with both hands, yanking it out of the stirrup.

"No!" Sir Charles dropped the reins in surprise, quickly losing his balance, the bag slipping through his fingers as he fell backward off the horse.

Lucas waited with open arms as the sack descended from the mare's neck, catching it before it dropped to the ground. "I've got you!"

"Oomph!"

Her sudden reaction reassured him that she was alert. He carefully lowered the bag and knelt on his knees. "Wait a moment. Let me get this untied."

"How dare you!" Sir Charles huffed as Edward pulled him to his feet, pinning both of his hands behind his back. "I want to see the local magistrate!"

"You are looking at him." Edward turned to Lucas. "How is she?"

He managed to loosen the string. The sack popped open. Emma thrust her head through the opening.

"*Whoosh!*" Her breath came out in one great gasp.

He put one arm around her as he gently brushed the tangled mass of hair off her face. "You are safe now, my darling."

Her brown eyes studied him as she took several more harried breaths. "You!"

He turned to Edward. "I'll take care of her. Make certain he never sets foot on British soil again."

"No! You can't do such a thing to me!" Sir Charles whined.

"As a matter of fact, there is an acquaintance of mine who is a ship's captain. He is sailing for Australia in a few days," Edward replied, triumphantly.

"Excellent." Lucas smiled at Emma as Edward led

the miscreant and the mare away. "You will never need to concern yourself with him anymore."

"I...I don't understand." She frowned at him.

"Didn't you hear what Edward said?" he reached in his coat pocket, pulled out his handkerchief, slowly and tenderly wiping the dirt marks off her cheeks.

"No. I am not referring to that." She struggled to sit up, pushing his hand away from her face. "I saw you kissing her."

"Ah." He grimaced as he put the cloth back inside his coat. "Actually, you saw a very drunk Lady Sophia force herself upon me."

Her eyes widened and she made an O shape with her delectable lips. "You aren't betrothed to her?"

He reached out, putting his hand on her shoulder, pulling her against his chest to kiss the top of her head. "Do you recall the bargain I made with you before we left Brighton? I intended to finish the conversations we started?"

"Yes."

"There is one discussion I am thinking of at this moment." He leaned back, smiling at her as he noted her confusion. "It covers two things I intend to speak of with you every day for the rest of our lives. Can you guess what I am referring to?"

A perplexed frown creased her forehead. "No. I'm sorry. I...I can't recall."

"You are forgiven for not being in top form at this moment, my dear." He grinned, taking her hand in his. "I am talking of *our love* and *our marriage*. I love you so very much. I want you to be my wife. I realize now I spent the last few years fighting a battle inside myself. I am well aware of my duty to my family, but I wanted more than an empty-headed shape of a woman sitting at the foot of my table or warming my bed. I believed I wanted love, but that notion made me apprehensive and confused. I certainly never experienced that kind of emotion before.

"Then I saw you, that first time, calmly holding your own when the starving youth attempted to rob you. You were affronted I offered you my assistance. I greatly enjoyed our brief, lively exchange. Then came the day I happened upon your nephews." He gently squeezed her hand. "I remember looking up while I held those two naughty lads by their collars, to see you standing at the side of the road. I recognized you immediately. My heart started pounding so loudly I could hear the vibration in my ears. I experienced a warm sensation in my chest, as if I swallowed the finest French brandy. Then, when I admitted to myself you were most probably the boys' mother, my heart literally plummeted to my stomach. I experienced extreme disappointment. I recall needing to gasp for air.

"Of course, at the time, I didn't recognize the symptoms for what they were. I just assumed I experienced a heightened reaction to all the craziness on the street and the near-disaster I averted."

Emma chuckled, blushing. "You certainly surprised me when you turned my hand over and rubbed the inside of my wrist with your thumb when you said goodbye."

He released her hand to wrap his arms around her once more. "Ah, yes. I couldn't help myself. Certainly, that was a symptom of the elation I experienced when I heard you were not married."

She hugged him back and then pulled away, looking up at him with shining eyes. "I love you so much, Lucas.

Thank you for always treating me with respect, never as an object of ridicule."

He sighed. "Oh, my love, my darling, understand you will never be exposed to such cruel treatment again."

She wrapped her arms around his neck, gazing tenderly at him. "Now, I want to make a bargain of my own."

"Ask me for anything you wish, my Emma," he replied, with a grin.

"When we are married," she paused, taking a deep breath before continuing. "Will you kiss me every morning and every night? Your kisses are wonderful."

"That is a request I would gladly agree to." He looked up at the sky for a moment. "It is afternoon, but why not add that to the list as well?"

She laughed. "I believe I am getting the better bargain."

"I disagree. This arrangement is of great benefit to us both." He leaned over to place his lips on hers.

Author's Notes

The descriptions of the exterior and interior of The Royal Pavilion, Brighton in this story were made from my own experience when I visited there in the early 1990s, supplemented by the book, *The Royal Pavilion, Brighton*, written by John Dinkel, copyright 1983.

The billiard game I described would not have happened in the Regency period. At that time, the game was played with white, ivory cue balls for each player and one red target ball.

Here is an excerpt from the next book in the Road To Romance Series, *Banished To Berkshire*.

A chilly breeze pulled at loose strands of her hair. She looked up at the sky. Dark, gray clouds scuttled by overhead. Standing up and wrapping her shawl tightly across her shoulders, she strode up the hill toward the back of the house.

"Lady Sophia! I wish to speak to you." Sir Edward rode across the upper pathway in the push chair as John guided him from behind. Peter guided their forward progress in front.

"John, Peter, go find something to do in the stables for a time," he ordered.

"What is it?" she asked as the two men walked away, impatient to return to her room, far away from his unsettling presence.

"I wanted to tell you, I am sorry," he replied.

She could feel the fiery, red blush coursing across her cheeks. She forced herself to speak. "I am not surprised. It is distressing to embrace an unrefined, tainted woman such as I."

He gasped. "I am not remorseful for the kisses we shared. It was a wondrous experience that I will always remember and cherish. Rather, I regret securing such gratification from you when I have the knowledge of your past abhorrent, emotional ordeal."

"Oh." She paused, mentally reviewing his comments with surprise. "Did I understand you correctly, you used the word *wondrous*?"

"Yes, truly extraordinary, as a matter of fact." He grinned at her.

"When…when you wrenched away," she halted, considering her next words. "I thought you were disgusted."

"Never!" His brilliant green eyes widened. "It is my turn to question your choice of words. The embrace brought me great pleasure and delight. Nothing regarding you could ever be cause for revulsion."

"Thank you." Feeling humbled and bewildered, she forced herself to smile.

"I want you to understand," he paused, studying her. "I will always be your friend. After we both leave here, if you ever need my assistance, no matter how trifling, please write to me at Horsham House."

"Oh!" His sincere, caring manner caused her to experience a warm, tingling sensation in the region of her heart. She couldn't come up with an ingenious reply.

"I greatly admire the intention to set up your own household," he continued. "I comprehend the constant struggle and many obstacles a woman must overcome when she determines to claim her independence and not marry. I applaud your tenacity."

"I appreciate your generous words and your faith in my abilities," she responded. "I am considering how best to tell my family of my plans."

"I advise you to secure your living arrangements before speaking to them," he remarked. "You will need to engage a companion as well."

She frowned. "Are you saying I should let a house in London without my father's knowledge?"

"Yes. I am guessing your family will forbid you from following through on the contemplation if you approach them with a representation of your plans initially. Do you have the funds needed to let a cottage or small house?"

"I...I believe so." She pondered on the probable sum required.

"Is there an elderly relation with no family of her own who could be asked to reside with you?"

She grimaced. "I have an unmarried cousin in her forties living in Bath and an elderly aunt, one of my father's sisters, with no other family in Canterbury."

"Both sound like good prospects," he assured her. "Letting a small house in London would cost approximately twenty pounds per year. Of course, you will need a footman, cook, housemaid. The price of coal runs about forty pounds yearly for a modest residence. If you could afford the additional cost of a coach and two horses requiring a coachman to drive, wages for all the help would be about seventy pounds a year and sixty-five pounds yearly for care of the animals and upkeep on the carriage."

"My goodness!" Her head spun with various sums. "I require approximately five hundred pounds yearly, then?"

"At a minimum," he advised. "I believe eight hundred to one thousand pounds yearly would see you settled quite comfortably. Remember, you will be required to feed and house the servants as well as yourself and your companion."

"A coach and horses are a luxury I do not believe I could afford," she told him with a frown. "Stables and rooms for the coachman and groom to sleep would mean a larger house and additional letting costs."

"Not necessarily," he rejoined. "If there are mews

close by, you can pay a fee to keep a coach and horses there. Learn what the choices and costs are before deciding against keeping a vehicle. I could write to my banker in London and ask him to look into available homes."

"Thank you for your offer, but I must decline," she countered. "I would not presume upon you to do such a thing for me."

"I assure you it is not an imposition," he assured her. "It only requires my request for the information. I will say my mother and sister are interested in acquiring their own abode if it would make you more comfortable."

"Very well." She studied him. "You are quite knowledgeable of the various aspects of owning a house in London."

"Do I shock you with the breadth of my understanding?" He chuckled. "I own a townhouse on Charles Street in Mayfair just down from Berkeley Square."

She gasped. "You do?"

"Yes. I visit London a few times a year," he informed her. "My mother and sister spend several months there. It made sense to purchase a house we could all live in when we stay in the city."

"How very wonderful and convenient. I remember Camille mentioning her visits to London when we were in finishing school together. I assumed she stayed with an older relative."

"Perhaps my mother and sister could accompany you on your search for a residence," he suggested. "I am certain they plan to return to London soon."

"Your mother has very good reason not to think kindly of me after I took the liberty of inviting Sir

Raeford to the party last summer without her prior consent," she reminded him, turning away to stare at some stalks of green beans growing at the edge of the kitchen garden. "I have no idea how much longer I will be sequestered here."

"Ah, yes, I forgot that awkward occasion and your indefinite sojourn." He sighed. "Here come John and Peter to escort me back to my room. I admit I am weary."

She whirled around to face him. "Oh, I am sorry! I should not have kept you talking for so long."

He grinned at her. "You mistake the matter. I requested your attendance and gladly participated in the discussion. Do not forget, we are friends. If you ever need anything, get in touch with me."

"I will remember. Thank you." She trained her gaze on the back of his head as the two men pushed him away from her, down the long pathway to the house.

A word about the author...

Cynthia Moore grew up in a small, southern California beach town. While many hours were spent lying on the sand, she always had a book in hand, or a paperback tucked inside a bag ready to pull out and read after a quick splash in the waves. Cynthia discovered British literature as a teenager. After reading most of the Victorian classics, she was introduced to English Regency period novels in 1987. It was love at first read. Since that time, Cynthia has read over four thousand fiction novels and owns a large collection of research books about the fascinating era. She is extremely proud to have several published stories set during the Regency and resides in Southern California with her dog who is, not surprisingly, named Austen.

Thank you for purchasing
this publication of The Wild Rose Press, Inc.

For questions or more information
contact us at
info@thewildrosepress.com.

The Wild Rose Press, Inc.
www.thewildrosepress.com

www.ingramcontent.com/pod-product-compliance
Lightning Source LLC
Chambersburg PA
CBHW070448260626
47161CB00004B/1241